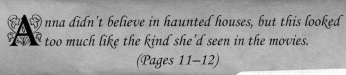

Anna didn't believe in haunted houses, but this looked too much like the kind she'd seen in the movies.
(Pages 11–12)

PASSAGES™
DARIEN'S RISE

Desert

LIZAB

KRAWLE

ADRIA

Territory

The Wilderness

RAUNDAL

Cannon Factory

DORR

MONROVIA

Field of the Gre

LEAPFORD

Darien's Family

GOTTHARD

Great Canyon

KELLEN

Forests of Gotthard

MUIRK

Mining Camp ←

PALATIA

Palatian King's Cottage

Age of Apostacy	Timeline = 2000 years		
	Arin		Glennall
	II		IV

FANGETALL

ALBANY

EASTCLIFF

Albany Road

The Downs

SARUM

US

hailsham

ge's
se

Arinshill

N
W E
S

Legend

— River
– – – Road
+++++ Railroad

GLENDALE

ley of the Rocks

FURNCHANCE

Mines

General's House

Caves of Laurel

Fendar | Period of the Judges | BOOK 1 DARIEN | Draven | Annison

VI | I | V | III

"Quickly now!" the young man commanded Kyle. They shuffled to the corner of the building, where they leaped to an adjoining roof.

(Page 20)

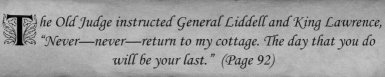

The Old Judge instructed General Liddell and King Lawrence, "Never—never—return to my cottage. The day that you do will be your last." *(Page 92)*

Suddenly there was a loud click and a hissing sound, followed by the arrow springing from the crossbow.
(Page 70)

aking a deep breath, Darien stepped out into the open. He didn't know what he had expected. But Darien certainly hadn't expected this . . . *(Page 144)*

Kyle looked a second time, not believing what he was seeing. The sky held two moons.

(Page 21)

When Anna and Kyle stumble into the beautiful and mysterious world of Marus, they find themselves drawn into a conflict with world-changing consequences. Caught in the middle of a nation-breaking feud, Anna and Kyle will be stretched to the brink. Will their newfound powers and wisdom be enough? And will they ever find their way home? Turning the pages of *Darien's Rise* is the only way to find out.

> **—Wayne Thomas Batson**
> Bestselling author of THE DOOR WITHIN TRILOGY: *Isle of Swords, Isle of Fire,* and *Curse of the Spider King*

PASSAGES isn't just a good read, it's an exhilarating ride through the world of Odyssey and into a parallel realm ripe with adventure, suspense, biblical allegory, and pure imagination. This is storytelling at its best.

> **—The Miller Brothers**
> Award-winning authors of *Hunter Brown and the Secret of the Shadow*

Biblical truths wrapped up in a wonderful mixture of adventure and page-turning suspense.

> **—Bill Myers**
> Author of the MY LIFE AS . . . series

What fun it is to realize that one character in PASSAGES represents a real person in the Bible. New insight opens up as the reader walks with a child from Odyssey in the world of Marus. And there's more: a mystery carried from book one to six!

> **—Donita K. Paul**
> Author of the DRAGON KEEPER CHRONICLES

I love this series of books because you can find a similar Bible story. This is a great book for people who love adventure.

    —Isaac H., age 10
    Colorado Springs, Colorado

The exciting, heart-beating, touching, one-of-a-kind book series—PASSAGES! Read it today!

    —Emma J., age 11
    Urbana, Illinois

The PASSAGES books are so great! . . . I really like how they [are about] kids from Odyssey who've been exported to another world . . . If you enjoy books about other world but can't seem to find any that are clean and spiritually uplifting, PASSAGES is the series for you.

    —Christian A., age 14
    Martin, Tennessee

I listened to PASSAGES: *Darien's Rise,* and I really enjoyed it! It was really good, and I could relate to Anna in so many ways! PS My dad liked it too.

    —Darci E., age 14
    Goodfield, Illinois

PASSAGES is now one of my favorite series. When I was reading them, I felt like I was there with the characters.

    —Grace O., age 14
    Mazomanie, Wisconsin

Adventures in Odyssey Presents
Passages, Book I

PASSAGES™

BOOK I

DARIEN'S RISE

by

Paul McCusker

Adventures in Odyssey®

TYNDALE

Tyndale House Publishers, Inc. • Carol Stream • Illinois

A Focus on the Family book published by
Tyndale House Publishers, Inc., Carol Stream, Illinois 60188

Editors: Larry Weeden and Mick Silva
Cover design, cover illustration, and interior illustrations by Mike Harrigan

Library of Congress Cataloging-in-Publication Data

McCusker, Paul,
    Darien's rise / by Paul McCusker.

    p. cm.

    Summary: Kyle and his sister Anna find themselves in an alternate world in
    which they have special powers to help carry out the will of the Unseen One.

    ISBN: 978-1-58997-613-9

    [1. Time and space Fiction. 2. Brothers and sisters Fiction.
    3. Christian life Fiction.] I. Title.

PZ7.M47841635Vo   1999

[Fic]—dc21   99-14208

                        CIP

Printed in the United States of America

1 2 3 4 5 6 7 8 9/ 15 14 13 12 11 10

For manufacturing information regarding this product, please call 1-800-323-9400.

For my brother Dan,
with love.
There. Are you happy now?

The winter rain fell like cold splinters on Odyssey. John Avery Whittaker, or *Whit* as he is best known, stood at the front window of Whit's End, his popular soda shop and discovery emporium. He watched the drops hit the grass that stretched out to the street. Cars splashed past. Men and women with large overcoats and billowing umbrellas crouched as they walked up and down the sidewalk. The grayness washed all color out of the day.

I won't get a lot of kids asking for ice cream today, he said to himself. He decided to get out an extra supply of hot chocolate mix.

One man suddenly ducked from the main street and made his way up the sidewalk to the front door of the shop. He burrowed deep into his coat to brace himself against the rain. One hand struggled with an umbrella. His other hand clutched a large, brown envelope. Whit smiled. It was Jack Allen, a childhood friend who now ran an antique shop in Odyssey. Whit was always glad to spend time with Jack.

The small bell above the door jingled as Jack opened it and stepped in from the cold. "My word!" he said when he saw Whit by the window. "It's a mess out there."

"Hi, Jack," Whit said. He walked over to the counter to fetch his friend something hot to drink. "What in the world are you doing out on a day like this?"

"I wanted to see you." Jack closed his umbrella and leaned it against the wall. He took off his coat, shook some water from it, then hung it on the rack that stood next to the door.

"Drink?" Whit held up a mug.

Jack nodded. "Coffee, please."

Whit poured a mug for each of them. As he did, Jack sat down at the counter and dropped the envelope onto the marble top.

"What's that?" Whit asked.

"A manuscript I thought you'd be interested in."

Whit gave Jack his mug of coffee. "A manuscript?" he asked.

"I found it in an old trunk I bought at an estate sale," Jack explained. "You remember the McCutcheons, don't you?"

"Sure. Mrs. McCutcheon used to teach English at the middle school. She was a wonderful woman. Taught for nearly 50 years, I think. Passed away a month and a half ago." Whit smiled fondly as he remembered Maude McCutcheon. She was a kind and dedicated teacher, loved by everyone in Odyssey.

"Her family decided to sell the house and almost everything in it. I went out yesterday for the auction. I bought some of the furniture, a few lamps and end tables, tapestries, and an old trunk from her attic." Jack sipped his coffee. "The trunk was filled with old clothes, a few books, the usual odds and ends. Nothing remarkable—except this manuscript."

"You think it's remarkable?" Whit asked.

Jack gazed at his friend. "I'd like you to read it and tell me what you think."

Whit opened the envelope and pulled out a thick notebook. The front of it had a standard black cover with a white panel in the center that said simply, "School Notebook." It was bound in black adhesive on the spine.

"It's a school book?" Whit said curiously. He opened the cover and saw page after page of neatly scripted handwriting on lined paper. "Somebody's class assignment?"

Jack shook his head. "That's what I thought until I read it. Now I'm not so sure."

In the upper-right-hand corner of the first page was written the date: October 3, 1958. Whit couldn't think of anything significant about the date. To the left, the author had written, "Chronicle of the Chosen."

Whit looked at Jack. "That's an interesting name."

"Just wait until you read the story."

"Ah!" Whit exclaimed, as if Jack had just given him an

important clue. "It's a story. Fiction or nonfiction?"

"You tell me after you read it."

"Is there an author? Do you know who wrote it?"

Jack smiled at him mischievously. "I won't say a word about it. Just read it."

"Okay, I'm hooked," Whit said with a smile. "I'll read it tonight."

By the time Whit got home from the shop that evening, the rain had turned to a beautiful snow. It fell in heavy white flakes. The weatherman on the radio called for a couple of feet of it to settle by morning. Whit guessed that the roads around town would be impassable by then. No doubt the businesses would shut down the next day and the children would get the day off from school. Even as an adult, he loved days like that. He felt a delightful sense of peace and security when he was forced to stay at home on cold wintry mornings. Then again, he might pull out his sled and join the kids who were sure to be playing on Bennigan Hill after breakfast.

Whit ate dinner, then made his way to the living room. He started a fire in the fireplace, got it to a satisfying heat, and sat down in his favorite chair with a cup of hot tea and the envelope Jack had given him. He opened the notebook and read once again, "The Chronicle of the Chosen."

"This isn't a child's handwriting," he said thoughtfully to no one. The handwriting gave Whit the impression of maturity: a formal style of penmanship resulting from an old-fashioned, classical education.

"Kyle and Anna pressed on through the thick green forest," the story began. . . .

CHAPTER

1

"**C**ome on!" Kyle ordered his younger sister impatiently. Anna had been snagged by the wild underbrush. "I'm going as fast as I can," she insisted. "Why don't they have paths in these woods?"

"Because they're old woods, and nobody comes here anymore," Kyle answered. "You remember what Uncle Bill said. Now hurry up!"

"Uncle Bill might have been pulling our leg," Anna said. She broke free from the underbrush. Old twigs snapped like firecrackers under her feet. "Slow down, Kyle!" she called as she raced to catch up.

Kyle slowed a little, but not enough for Anna to notice. He was a stubborn 12-year-old who would never openly concede to doing something nice for his 10-year-old sister.

She puffed irritably behind him. "I knew this would happen," she said. "I should have stayed with Grandma."

"And get bored stiff," Kyle reminded her.

Anna didn't respond. Kyle was right. Since they'd come to Odyssey to stay with their grandparents at the beginning of the summer, they'd been bored. As a couple of "city kids," they found it hard to cope with the slower pace and less-sophisticated pleasures of a small town. Their grandparents did their best to keep the two kids active, but there was only so much that could hold their interest. Kyle and Anna finally admitted to themselves that they'd made a big mistake when they let their parents talk them into going to Odyssey for a month.

A glimmer of hope arose, however, when their Uncle Bill came to visit just last evening and told them about an old, mysterious house in the middle of the woods. He said it had been empty for years. Some said it was haunted, others that it was magical, while still others claimed it once belonged to an eighteenth-century pirate who'd buried his treasure in the garden. "Whatever it is," Uncle Bill said, "it might be a fun way to pass the time."

Both Grandma and Grandpa pooh-poohed the story. Neither of them could remember an old house in the woods. But Uncle Bill insisted it was there, not far from Darien's Creek in what they called the Black Forest.

Kyle was immediately intrigued and wanted Uncle Bill to draw a map. Uncle Bill scribbled directions as well as he could remember them—he hadn't been there since he was a child, he admitted. Kyle said he would go the next day if it was all right with his grandparents.

"Sure, you can go," his grandfather said. "But you won't find anything."

Anna didn't agree to go with Kyle until the next morning. She didn't really want to, but she thought it would be better than holding Grandma's yarn while she knitted. Now—in the middle of the hot and humid Black Forest—she thought of that yarn and a tall glass of lemonade and wished she'd stayed behind in spite of the boredom.

Kyle tripped on a rock and fell, getting covered in dark mulch. Dead leaves stuck to his close-cropped, blond hair.

Two circles of wet dirt formed on the knees of his jeans. "I'll bet nobody's walked through here in years," he said happily.

Anna didn't understand her brother. How could he be happy? It upset her to discover that her white sneakers were now a spotted brown. Her pants were streaked and smudged with dirt and decaying bark. She had torn the sleeve on her shirt. This expedition was turning into a disaster as far as she was concerned.

And what would they do if they didn't find a house? Worse, she thought, what if they did find it and it was all the things Uncle Bill had said? Maybe that pirate still haunted the house, scaring away strangers who hoped to dig up his treasure.

"That would be cool!" Kyle said when Anna told him her worries.

No, she didn't understand her brother at all.

Half an hour later, she was beyond trying to understand him and openly complained that it was time to go home. "The house doesn't exist," she said. "Uncle Bill was just teasing us."

Kyle wouldn't hear of it. "It's around here somewhere. It has to be."

Another half hour went by, and Anna began to worry out loud that they were lost.

"We're not lost!" Kyle snapped. "I never should have let you come along. All you do is gripe, gripe, gripe!"

"I want to go home," she said and abruptly sat down right where she was. "I'm tired and thirsty."

Kyle towered over her with his hands on his hips. "Then go home," he told her. "I don't care."

"I'll get lost," she said.

"That's not my problem."

"It will be if Mom and Dad find out you let me wander around alone in some strange woods."

He groaned.

"You know I'm right."

"You really get on my nerves," he said with a frown.

"That makes us even."

"Yeah, sure." Kyle glanced ahead longingly. He wanted to go on. But he had to admit—not out loud, though—that he was getting tired too. He sighed deeply, then said casually, "Okay, let's go back. But first you'd better knock that bug out of your hair."

Anna had long, thick, brown hair and lived in horror that a bug would hide in it somewhere. One night before bed, she had brushed a small spider out of it. She had screamed loudly enough to wake up the neighbors. The police had come. She'd had nightmares for a week.

If there had been any sleeping neighbors in these woods—or police—the situation would have repeated itself. She screamed out one long note, leaped to her feet, and danced wildly while flicking her hair with both hands. "Get it out! Get it out!" she shrieked.

Of course the bug flew away the instant Anna moved, but that didn't stop her from screaming, dancing, and flicking for a full seven minutes.

As Kyle tried to calm her down, he caught a glimpse of the house through the trees.

———⚜———

"This is incredible!" Kyle exclaimed. "I told you we'd find it!"

The house stood awkwardly in an area so thick with trees that the sunlight couldn't break through. It looked completely out of place.

"What's it doing here?" Anna whispered. "It's like it got lost from all the other houses and died here. Why would anyone want to build a house in the middle of nowhere?"

"I don't know," Kyle said breathlessly as he circled around to the front. It was everything Uncle Bill had said: big, empty, and mysterious. Part of it reminded him of an English castle, with walls made of large blocks of uncut stone and a tower sticking up from the corner. It had round, arched windows leading up to a conelike roof. Then it was as if the builder had gotten bored with that idea and decided to do something else. The rest of the house looked Gothic, with decorative gables, ornamental shingles, and shuttered windows jutting out of long walls. The porch was framed by intricate molding on the rails between the slim posts. It surrounded three sides of the house as if it were a belt meant to hold it all together.

Kyle's imagination went wild with images of pirates, secret meetings, and treasure. "Maybe Darien's Creek used to be a big river that led to the sea," he said. "I'll bet the pirates brought their ships in and hid here."

"Pirates?" Anna asked with a loud gulp. She hadn't forgotten the image of the ghost of a captain protecting his booty.

They slowly approached the steps leading up to the long front porch. Closer now, they could see how dark and dirty the place was. Windows were broken out. A tree had fallen and smashed through a wall on the far side. Portions of the roof had collapsed, the wood having given up its strength and decomposed a long time ago. Kyle reached the front door. It was made of heavy wood, worn and scarred, with panels of glazed glass, most of which were shattered.

"This is great!" Kyle said.

Anna lingered behind. She didn't believe in haunted

houses, but this looked too much like the kind she'd seen in the movies.

"I don't like it," she groaned. "Let's go home." She knew Kyle wouldn't listen to her. He never listened to her. Nobody did, as far as she was concerned. She was just a little girl without a voice.

He tried the door handle. It turned, and the door opened with a loud creaking sound. Kyle winced at the smells of rotten wood, mold, and animal droppings.

Anna stayed by the steps. "Kyle!" she called.

"Stay out here if you want to," he said. He was turned away from her, so she couldn't see his wry smile. "I'm sure the bugs will leave your hair alone."

Anna hurried to Kyle's side and held on to his arm.

The house looked as bad on the inside as it did on the outside. Cobwebs clung to the corners of the cracked ceiling and chipped plaster walls. Black smudges outlined the places where framed pictures had once hung. Leaves swirled and spread across the floor like brown fairies. Nests of branches and bush filled some of the corners and the fireplaces.

"Cool," Kyle whispered.

The lower floor was made up of what was once a spacious living room, a library (with collapsed bookshelves), a dining room that led into what must have been the kitchen, and a small pantry. After their tour, Anna insisted that they go home.

"Not yet," Kyle said. "Not until I see the whole house." He started walking up the stairs. They protested with creaks and groans.

Anna looked around nervously and knew they'd made a mistake. They shouldn't have come here. Why didn't Uncle Bill learn to keep his mouth closed? Why couldn't she make

Kyle listen to her?

"Hey! Is anybody here?" Kyle suddenly called out when they reached the top of the stairs.

Anna jumped. "Are you trying to give me a heart attack?" she protested.

"Do you hear that?" he asked her softly, cocking his ear.

"Hear what?"

He hesitated as he listened again. "Voices. I hear someone talking."

"You're trying to scare me," Anna said nervously.

"No, I'm serious," Kyle said, then crept along the second floor. "Back here."

"I don't hear anything."

They passed a couple of open doors that led into what were probably bedrooms. Their condition was the same as that of the rooms on the first floor.

"I don't like this," Anna whispered again. The floor beneath her felt wobbly. They were walking on loose boards. Kyle ignored her and pressed on down the corridor. He stopped at a closed door.

"In here," Kyle said softly. Putting his ear against the rotten wood, he listened, then whispered, "Someone's in here."

Anna watched her brother carefully. Was he teasing her, or had he been out in the woods too long?

"Can't you hear them?"

"No," she replied sullenly.

Kyle shot her an annoyed look, then knelt down and peeked in the keyhole. His eyes grew wider than she'd ever seen them. He gasped. "There are people in there!"

"Cut it out, Kyle," she demanded. "You're not funny." All her instincts told her to run away as fast as she could. But she didn't dare. She knew he'd never stop teasing her for falling for his joke.

He continued in a low whisper, "It's so weird! They're dressed in old-fashioned clothes. Like . . . like . . . uniforms and . . ." He couldn't find the words to describe it and gave up. "The room is full of furniture and paintings and . . ." His voice trailed off. "This doesn't make any sense. How can there be a room like this in an abandoned house?"

Anna tugged at his arm. "Let's get out of here!" she begged.

"But you have to see this," he insisted.

"I don't care! Let's go before we get in trouble!"

"Look first. I want to prove I'm not crazy." He stepped back so she could see into the keyhole.

Anna figured the only way to get Kyle out of the house was to do what he said. She bent down to look. At first she didn't see anything. She squinted and looked again. The room was there, but it was as empty and run-down as the rest of the house. "I don't see anything," she said.

"Look harder!" Kyle whispered.

She did. The room was still empty and run-down. "Kyle—" she began to say.

Suddenly they heard a loud crack. The floorboards beneath Kyle's feet buckled, then gave way. Kyle shouted as he fell backward. His hands clawed at the air. Anna reached for him, but it was too late. He crashed through the floor.

Anna crawled on her hands and knees to the edge of the gaping hole of old wood and splinters. "Kyle!" she screamed.

She couldn't see below. The hole was black except for a swirling cloud that Anna thought was dust from the ceiling plaster. The cloud spun around and around but didn't clear. If Kyle was down there, Anna couldn't figure out where he was.

"Kyle! Are you all right?" she called out. He didn't answer. Certain he was hurt, Anna got to her feet to run to the stairs. The floorboards in front of her also cracked loudly. *The whole floor is going to cave in,* she thought. She stepped back, pressed herself against the wall, then slid along to the closed bedroom door. "Kyle!" she cried.

She felt for the doorknob and prayed it wasn't locked, suddenly desperate for someplace safe. It turned easily. She pushed the door open and carefully inched backward into the room, turned on her heel to walk in, and was suddenly engulfed in a bright, white light.

Nobody ever listens to me was the last thing she thought before the light drew her in.

Kyle instantly realized three things. First, he knew that he'd fallen through the floor but hadn't landed on the ground below. He was in a sitting position, leaning against something hard. Second, he couldn't see anything because he was wrapped up in a large cloth. Third, he heard the distinct sound of a sword fight going on somewhere nearby. He was by no means an expert on sword fighting—all he knew he'd seen at the movies—but the sound of men's grunts and the *ching* of the sabers hitting each other was unmistakable.

He struggled to free himself from the cloth entangling him. He pushed hard with his arms in both directions and felt the fabric loosen. Another push, then one more, and he was uncovered. His mouth fell open at what he saw. Two men were sword fighting in the center of an ornate study. One was silver-haired with a thick mustache. He wore an impressive navy-blue uniform with epaulets and gold stitching around the sleeves. The other was much younger, with curly dark hair and a slender, clean-shaven face. He was dressed in a loose white shirt and old-fashioned breeches that tucked into his black boots.

Kyle stood up. With a glance, he realized he had been sitting behind a thick velvet curtain, his back to a wall containing an open window. It was night outside. *What in the world is going on here?* he wondered as he watched the two men fight. One thing was certain: The men were not practicing. With each thrust and parry, one tried to wound the other.

"No one needs to get hurt," the younger man said. "I want only your medals."

The older man wheezed as he dodged the younger man's sword and said, "And I want only your head!"

Several voices shouted from the hallway, "Commander! Commander!" Someone pounded on the closed door to the study. The handle turned rapidly but didn't open. The pounding grew more fierce. *They're going to break the door down,* Kyle feared.

With quick thrusts, the younger man drove the older man across the room until he was trapped against the large white marble fireplace. The fire in it popped and crackled, the flames threatening to lick the heels of the older man's boots. The younger man suddenly grabbed the older man's sword-fighting arm and banged it against the mantel with such force that the sword fell from his hand.

Pressing the point of his sword against the older man's throat, the younger man said breathlessly, "And now, your medal, please?"

The older man growled, "You dishonor yourself, sir."

"It wouldn't be the first time," the younger man answered with a laugh.

Seeing that he had no choice, the older man grabbed the medal on his chest and tore it from his jacket. "I hope you are satisfied," he said as he thrust the medal into the younger man's hand.

"Completely," the young man said. "Now, if you'll forgive me . . ." He grabbed a vase from the mantel and hit the older man across the head with it. The older man fell to the floor. "I'm so sorry," the younger man said sincerely. With a light step, he spun toward the window and saw Kyle for the first time. He held up his saber. "Hello, lad," he said. "I didn't see you there. Please thank your master for his hospitality."

"He's not my master," Kyle said. For some reason, he wasn't afraid of the swordsman. "I don't even know what I'm doing here."

The pounding at the door grew more rhythmic. The men were obviously throwing their full weight against it in unison. The wood began to crack around the frame.

"You had better figure it out soon," the young man said. "I don't think our friends on the other side of the door will take kindly to strangers."

Kyle felt a sick feeling in his stomach and looked at the door, just in time to see the older man silently struggle to his feet. He had a fire poker in his hand, and suddenly he lunged at the younger man's back. "Watch out!" Kyle shouted.

The young man swung around, raising his guard just in time to stab the older man in the side. The older man dropped the poker and fell to his knees, clutching his wound.

"Blast!" the younger man said with irritation. "I told you I didn't want anyone to get hurt."

The older man cursed at him.

At the window, the young man sheathed his sword and leaned toward Kyle. "You saved my life, and I thank you," he said. "Now, if you have no specific plans, I suggest you come with me."

"To where?" Kyle asked.

"Anywhere but here," the young man said with a smile and stepped through the window onto the ledge. Kyle followed instinctively.

"Whoa!" Kyle said when he saw that they were on the second floor.

Soldiers were gathering on the patio below, holding torches in their hands. One pointed up at them and shouted, "There!"

"Keep moving and don't look down," the young man said to Kyle. The ledge was only about half a foot wide, and they had to balance themselves carefully against the wall as they crept along the side of the mansion.

One of the soldiers fired a pistol at them. Chunks of granite sprayed the side of Kyle's face. "Ouch!" he cried.

The young man reached behind his back and produced a small handgun. He fired a couple of shots down toward the soldiers, apparently not to hit them but only to make them scatter. They did so with a lot of shouts and rude exclamations.

"Quickly now!" the young man commanded.

They shuffled to the corner of the building, where they leaped to an adjoining roof. Catlike, they raced along the roof, around another section of the house, and then jumped to the top of a small building. Kyle noticed that this building seemed to be part of a large wall separating the mansion and its gardens from a forest. Somewhere the soldiers were shouting things like, "I think he went this way!" and "No, over here!" But their voices grew distant as the young man led Kyle along a dark stretch of the wall. The young man then knelt down and swung himself from the top of the wall to a horse waiting below. Kyle hesitated.

"Come on, lad," the young man said. "You can be sure you're not welcome here."

Kyle crawled over the side of the wall. With helping hands from the young man, he landed behind him on the horse.

"Put your arms around my waist and keep your head down!" the young man shouted over his shoulder. He then nudged the horse to get moving. They raced into the dark forest.

How the young man or the horse knew where they were going in the black woods, Kyle couldn't guess. He knew only to hold on tight and pray they wouldn't be scooped from the horse by a wayward branch or tripped up by a fallen tree. To his amazement, they weren't. After a couple of miles, they reached an incline. At the top, they were suddenly surrounded by a dozen men, also on horseback.

"Did you get them, General?" one of the men asked as he saluted.

"I did," the young man said with a hearty laugh. "Is the train ready?"

"This way," another man said—and they were all off again.

As they rode through another forest, Kyle wondered, *Where is this place? Have I stumbled onto some strange section of Odyssey?* They splashed through a small brook and emerged into an open field. Something in the sky caught Kyle's attention: a brightness more luminous than any full moon he had ever seen. He looked a second time, not believing what he was seeing.

The sky held *two* moons. One was large and white, the other nearly half the size and slightly orange.

I'm not in Odyssey anymore, he thought.

Like Kyle, Anna found herself blinded. But she wasn't wrapped up in a curtain; she seemed to be in some sort of closet. *What happened?* she wondered. One minute she was staring into a bright white light, and the next she was sitting in thick darkness. Had she stepped into this strange place when she backed into the room? That didn't make sense. She had seen through the keyhole a big, empty *room,* not a closet. Had she fallen along with Kyle and was now unconscious and dreaming?

She pushed coats and other clothes aside and saw a sliver of light at the bottom of what was certainly a door. She reached for the handle and opened the door just a crack. She heard men's voices. She stopped, afraid of who the men might be. Maybe they were the men Kyle had seen through the keyhole.

Whoever they were, they didn't sound happy. They were in a full-blown shouting match. Anna tried to position herself to see what was going on. She caught a glimpse of one man pacing back and forth on a colorfully patterned carpet in front of several tall windows covered with white curtains. He was a large, older man with wild, brown hair and a heavy beard and mustache, all streaked with gray. His arms were clasped behind his back, except when he occasionally gestured frantically with his right hand. He had a set frown on his brow.

"I can't believe what I'm hearing!" the man shouted in a low, lionlike voice. "My own son plays the fool with me!"

Another man, this one much younger, stepped into view. He had all the looks of the older man, except he had nicely groomed, wavy hair and a thin mustache. Anna knew instantly that the young man was the son of the elder. Both were dressed in old-fashioned uniforms, the kind Anna had seen in her history textbooks. The coats had epaulets on the shoulders and an insignia of an eagle on their chests. She thought for a moment and remembered from historical movies she'd seen that men wore uniforms like that in England and Germany back in the late 1800s. She couldn't imagine why anyone would wear such clothes in 1958.

"Father, listen to reason," the son pleaded.

"Am I not the king?" the older man asked, gesturing wildly. "*King* Lawrence! Doesn't that mean anything to anyone? And aren't you my successor? Will you not be *King George* one day?"

The prince didn't answer. He leaned against a large wooden desk and folded his arms. His expression was one of weariness, as if he knew that there was no talking to his father when he got like this.

The king continued, "So what am I to think when the people of my nation talk about one of my generals as if *he* should be king instead of me? Eh? Answer me that!"

"You know how people are," Prince George appealed. "They're fickle. General Darien is everyone's hero now. People talk like that about their heroes."

"They once spoke about *me* that way—and I was made their king as a result!" The king slammed his fist against the desktop. "Don't you see it, boy? All Darien has to do is simply *hint* that he would like to be their king and we're done for! We'll have a revolution!"

Prince George shook his head and said, "But Darien wouldn't do that. Darien has no interest in being king. His allegiance is to you, Father. He knows you are the man selected by the Unseen One to be king of this country. He honors that. He honors you. Why else would he win so many victories against the Palatians in your name?"

"Your friendship with him has made you blind. He will betray me—and you—and our entire succession."

"Why worry about our family? With his impending

marriage to Princess Michelle, we'll all rule as a family any-way." Prince George drifted toward a large bookcase and looked as if he were going to choose a book from the shelf.

The king laughed without humor. "He'll marry Michelle *if* he fulfills his vow."

Prince George turned to him. "That was a ridiculous vow, and I'm sorry you let him go through with it. Imagine letting your best general risk his life to retrieve a few medals—"

"One hundred medals is not 'a few.' It will be quite impressive if he can get them without dying in the process."

"But to dare him like you did! What could he do but accept your dare?"

The king spread his arms. "Darien is a peasant at heart. To marry the daughter of royalty would have seemed above his station. He had to do something to prove him-self to us. Asking him to retrieve 100 Palatian medals seemed reasonable."

"Are you sure you weren't hoping he'd get killed along the way?"

The king looked deliberately at his son and said, "Whatever happens will be Darien's doing, not mine."

"But to go through all that for *Michelle,*" Prince George said, exasperated. "She's beneath him!"

"Be careful what you say about your own sister. She'll keep Darien in his place."

"Mary was the one for Darien, and you know it."

"I needed Mary to wed the prince of Albany. It was good politics and good for our nation's security. With Albany as an ally, we'll be much safer in the Northern Territories."

"It was unconscionable to promise Mary to Darien, then give her to Albany," Prince George persisted.

The king shrugged. "You'll learn one day that the king

must make many hard decisions for the sake of his people."

"It's interesting to me that you make these 'hard decisions' and they all seem designed to hurt Darien."

The king smiled wryly. "Is Darien not man enough to handle it?"

"Darien is a great man!" Prince George exclaimed sharply. "And he will be loyal to you no matter what you do to him."

"We'll see about that," the king replied.

Prince George faced his father and said softly, "You continually wrong a man who has done you no harm. There are others in your army who need closer watching."

"Like whom?"

Just then the phone on the desk rang, the bell loud and shrill. Prince George picked up the receiver. "Yes?" He paused, listened, then frowned. "Send him in."

A few seconds later, a uniformed man with short-cropped hair, handlebar mustache, and a scar on his cheek entered. "Sire," he said with a quick bow.

"General Liddell," the king said. "What news do you bring?"

"I've received word from the Palatian border that General Darien has successfully returned from his mission and is on his way home to the capital by train. He'll arrive here tomorrow."

The king's face turned red. "What?" he roared.

"That *is* good news!" Prince George said with an eye to his father. "Did he capture the 100 medals?"

"I don't know," General Liddell said as he moved toward the closet. Anna shrank back, afraid he would see her through the crack.

"I'm sure he did!" Prince George clapped his hands happily. "If you'll excuse me, Father, I'd like to make arrangements for a feast to celebrate Darien's return."

The king waved a dismissive hand at him. Prince George strode out, laughing as he went.

The king slammed his fist on the desk again furiously. "What will it take to get rid of this man?" he asked.

"What would you like me to do, my king?" General Liddell asked.

The two men gazed at each other for a moment. "There are things we can discuss," the king said.

General Liddell smiled. "I'm sure there are. You need only say the word."

King Lawrence gestured to his general. "Let's walk in the garden for a while."

The two men left.

Anna waited a moment and tried to sort out everything that had happened. It was more than she could cope with. Where was she? Who were these people? How did she get from an abandoned house in the middle of the woods to this fancy room?

It was a dream, she decided. And the best way back to the real world was to get out of this closet—and out of this house. She gently pushed the door open, peeked around to be sure she was alone, and tiptoed across the room. The décor was more awesome than she could see from the closet. There were busts on marble pedestals in every corner, large sofas and chairs with upholstery of intricate tapestry, glass-covered bookcases, and an enormous fireplace. An ornate clock chimed in the corner. She gaped at the room, wishing she had time to look it over more thoroughly. She opened the door slowly and stuck her head into the hall. Suddenly, large hands grabbed her roughly.

"Just as I suspected," General Liddell growled from

behind her. "A spy."

The king, who stood nearby, clucked his tongue. "However did you see her in the closet, General?" he said. "You're amazing."

"I'm not a spy!" Anna protested.

"Notice how oddly she's dressed," the king said, "as if she wishes to be disguised as a boy!"

Anna glanced down self-consciously at her blouse with the torn sleeve and her smudged pants. "I'm not disguised as a boy," she insisted. "These are *my* clothes." She added with a heartfelt plea, "You have to help me! I'm *lost*."

"Lost in the king's palace?" the general asked suspiciously. "How is that possible?"

In a torrent of words, Anna told the general and the king about Odyssey, the old house, and the bright white light. They laughed at her.

"Normally we put spies to death," General Liddell said.

Anna began to cry. "I didn't do anything wrong. I don't know how I got here!"

The king looked over Anna carefully, then told General Liddell, "Give her to Titus. He'll know what to do with her."

General Liddell pulled Anna through the palace, up and down several flights of stairs, and down a long, dark hallway until they were in a quiet, nearly deserted section. He opened a large, wooden door that led into a little-used courtyard. Across the dirty pavement, past a dry, cracked fountain, sat a broken-down shack. "Titus!" the general shouted.

Titus was as round as he was tall. His torn trousers and stained shirt could barely contain his enormous form. His jowls flapped when he spoke, and his bald head glimmered with sweat no matter what the temperature around him. When he smiled, which he only ever did cruelly, one noticed that half his teeth were missing. Anna's first impression was that he was the kind of man you would expect to sell little kids into slavery. Her impression was right. That's exactly what he did.

Titus bowed as low as his bulky frame would let him. "My general," he said.

"We found this trespasser in the king's study. Sell her as a slave," General Liddell ordered as he pushed Anna to the ground.

"Very good, sir. The dealers meet in the morning."

"Don't explain," General Liddell said. "Just see to it." He turned and left the same way he had come.

"Hello, little girl," Titus leered, then poked a finger at her pants. "Or are you a girl? You dress like a boy."

"It's a mistake!" Anna cried out.

Titus dragged Anna from the courtyard and down into a damp cellar that could be best described as a dungeon. The door even had bars on the window. He took her to a corner littered with moldy straw.

"You won't make me stay in here!" Anna cried. "Please don't make me stay in here!"

Titus laughed. Using rope, he tied her to an iron ring attached to the wall. "Night night," he said and marched out, slamming the large door behind him. He peeked through the barred window. "I wouldn't sleep much if I were you. The rats like to nibble."

Anna screamed.

CHAPTER

3

Kyle was on a steam train, the kind with an enormous chimney on top of the front engine. It puffed, whooshed, and whistled its way through the dark countryside. Kyle had followed the general—Darien was his name—onto the train, where the general told his entire regiment how Kyle had warned him about the fire poker and saved his life. The men gave Kyle extra-special consideration after that, offering him a hot meal and a comfortable berth in which to sleep. But sleep was the last thing Kyle wanted. He had dozens of questions about where he was and how he got there and who these people were. General Darien smiled at the boy and said they would talk after a good night's rest. Kyle was sure he'd never rest—until his head hit the pillow. He slept until dawn.

Kyle was awake before anyone else. He climbed down from the berth and discovered his clothes, washed and dried, hanging on a hook nearby. He put them on, then walked softly down the passageway. It stretched the length of the train car, with sleeping berths stacked up on both sides. He could hear some of the soldiers snoring behind the curtains that gave the small compartments their privacy.

A sentry stood guard at the end of the car. He eyed Kyle carefully, remembered who the boy was, and said that he

could get breakfast in the dining car, two cars ahead. Kyle
thanked him and stepped through the door into the chilly
morning air. He lingered there only a minute—just long
enough to be impressed with the beautiful green countryside
they rolled past. The train jolted, and Kyle decided he should
get into the next car. Unlike the previous car, with berths
stacked up along the passageway, this one had room-sized
compartments with doors. Apart from the rattle and hum of
the train itself, everything was quiet.

Kyle went through to the next car, where tables were set
up for dining, just as the sentry had said. A man in a white
jacket smiled at Kyle and gestured to a window seat at one
of the tables. Kyle sat down. Before he could say anything at
all, the man had placed a glass of orange juice and a glass of
milk in front of him.

"Compliments of the general," the man said. "He told me
to give you the full treatment."

Kyle liked being treated like a hero.

Light poured in through the window. Kyle craned his
neck to see if this world had more than one sun. He found
himself squinting at just one, which was rising on the horizon. But the fields and trees that lay in front of it seemed
somehow brighter, more vibrant, and greener than anything
he'd seen in Odyssey or the rest of his world. He leaned back
in the chair and wondered if it was a trick of the light or perhaps only his imagination.

The train whistle sounded as they passed through a station. Kyle looked out the window in time to see dozens of
people on the platform. Some waved and shouted enthusiastically. Others held signs saying things like "Hooray General
Darien!" and "General Darien, our hero."

"Wow," Kyle said to himself.

"They love him, you know," a man said to Kyle. Startled, Kyle looked over to the end of the table. The man standing there was dressed in a double-breasted gray uniform with medals on his chest. He had a wrinkled brow that made him look stern, though his face was young. He had wavy red hair and wore a goatee. The man pulled out a chair and sat down across the table from Kyle. "May I?" he asked after he'd already sat down. "I'm Colonel Oliver."

"I'm Kyle."

"Oh, I know who you are," Colonel Oliver said softly. "You're the boy who saved our general's life. And for that, we're eternally grateful. But I'd like to know who you really are and what you're up to."

The words came so fast and the tone stayed so pleasant that, for a moment, Kyle didn't catch on to what the colonel was saying. "Up to?" he asked.

"Don't toy with me, young man. How did you wind up in that room when the general was there?"

Kyle shook his head. "I don't know."

"You can do better than that."

"No, I'm serious—I don't know," Kyle said defensively. "One minute I was in an empty house, falling through the floorboards, and the next minute I was in that room. I don't know how it happened. See, I was visiting my grandparents in Odyssey, and my sister and I—"

Colonel Oliver held up a hand and said, "Spare me the details."

"I just wanted to explain that—"

"I knew you wouldn't answer directly." Colonel Oliver leaned forward on the table. "Be sure, boy, that I'll be keeping my eye on you. If you're really working for the Palatians, I'll find out about it. Even if you're not, I'm going to find out who and what you are."

A jovial voice called out from the doorway, "What he is? I'll tell you what he is, my dear colonel. He's my guardian angel!"

Colonel Oliver leaped to his feet and saluted.

General Darien stepped into the car and strode briskly to the table. He patted Kyle on the back. "Don't mind Colonel Oliver," he said kindly. "He's paid to be suspicious. It's what often keeps us all alive." Then, turning to the colonel, he said, "Thank you, Ollie."

Colonel Oliver understood the cue that he was expected to leave. He saluted again and, with one last glaring look at Kyle, walked over to a table at the opposite end of the car.

"Mind if I sit down?" General Darien asked.

"Yes . . . I mean, no. I mean, please sit down," Kyle said.

The general did and signaled to the waiter for a cup of coffee. "I only have a minute," he said. "Did you sleep well? Are you rested?"

"Yes, sir. Thank you."

"Good," the general said and fiddled with the buttons on his uniform. Like Colonel Oliver's, it was gray and heavily decorated with medals. "Sorry, but I can't stand to wear this thing. Uniforms give me a rash. Give me regular shirts and trousers any day." He smiled, and it almost seemed to Kyle that his teeth and eyes sparkled when he did. Kyle decided the general couldn't be much older than 25. He was like the older brother Kyle always wished he'd had—or would one day be.

The coffee arrived. General Darien dropped a splash of cream into it, then gazed at Kyle for a moment. "You don't look like a Palatian," he said. "And I wouldn't guess that you're from Marus, either."

"Marus? Where is Marus?" Kyle asked.

The general looked surprised. "You've never heard of Marus?"

"No, sir. Where is it?"

"You're riding through it, lad." The general chuckled. "Perhaps I should be quiet and allow you to tell me from where you've come. I'm curious—not suspicious, mind you, but curious."

Kyle drank his milk and ate a bowl of oatmeal and some toast with jam, all in the time it took to tell General Darien his story. The general asked one or two questions but didn't say anything otherwise. When Kyle finished, the general leaned back in his chair. "That's a remarkable story," he said.

"It's true!" Kyle said. He had no doubt that his story sounded crazy. It sounded crazy even to him.

The general rubbed his chin and told Kyle, "I've never heard of any of the places you say you're from. Explaining how you got here is probably impossible. I'd suggest it's all a dream, but you're real enough and so am I, so that knocks *that* out of our consideration." He thought for a moment. "When we have the chance, I'll take you to the Old Judge. He's wise about such things. Maybe he can explain it."

"I hope so," Kyle said. "I'm worried about my sister. She might get lost if she tries to find her way back to my grandparents. Oh—my grandparents! They'll be worried, too."

"Don't worry about it, Kyle. We're all in the hands of the Unseen One." Kyle wanted to ask who the Unseen One was, but the general stood up. "Meanwhile, you're my personal guest. It's the least I can do for the service you did for me. Now, if you'll excuse me, I have to meet with my officers. A boring business meeting." He winked and smiled as he left.

Later in the morning, Kyle came upon a group of boys in

another car who were polishing boots, cleaning pistols, and shining swords. They were cadets whose sole purpose at this stage of their life was to make sure the officers were catered to. Kyle was pleased to meet up with boys his own age. The adults were polite enough, but none of them besides the general had gone out of his way to speak to him.

The boys were extremely curious about Kyle and weren't shy about asking him more questions than he had answers for. Once again, he told his story about how he wound up in the Palatian general's mansion. They were silent as they listened and went about their work. Kyle couldn't tell if they believed him or not.

One of the boys finally said, "That's quite a story. I *hope* it's true. Otherwise you're one of the best liars I ever met."

Kyle protested that he wasn't a liar, but he knew it wouldn't make any difference. Why should anyone believe him?

"Since you've been asking me a lot of questions, do you mind if I ask you a few?" he said.

The boys said they didn't mind.

"For starters, where are we going?"

A fair-haired boy replied, "We're going to our capital. It's called Sarum. General Darien is taking back his 'prizes' "—at this the rest of the boys giggled—"from the Palatians. They're our enemies, by the way. And then the king will let General Darien marry his daughter."

"I don't understand," Kyle said. "General Darien went into enemy territory to bring back prizes so he could marry the king's daughter? If he's a general, why didn't the king just say yes?"

The fair-haired boy smiled indulgently and answered, "You honestly don't know *anything* about Marus, do you?"

"I really don't."

"Well," the boy began, "General Darien wasn't always a general. In fact, he wasn't even raised to be a soldier. A couple of years ago, he was just a farm boy out in one of the crop-growing counties. But after he killed Commander Soren—"

"Commander Soren?"

"He was Palatia's greatest leader," another boy interjected.

The fair-haired one continued. "Commander Soren and the Palatian army invaded—"

"As *usual*," the second boy said with mock boredom.

The fair-haired one shot him an impatient look. "Anyway, they had our army cornered near Glendale. That's a town in the southwest part of the country, near the mines. We rode past it in the middle of the night."

"He doesn't want a geography lesson," one of the other boys said, then spat on a boot to polish it.

The fair-haired boy went on. "The story goes that Darien and his brothers had decided to enlist in the army to battle the Palatians. They arrived at Glendale just when it looked as if King Lawrence was about to surrender to Soren.

"When Darien heard this, he was furious. He couldn't believe that the people of Marus would ever surrender to the Palatians, under any condition. He made such a fuss about it that an officer grabbed him and dragged him in front of the king to get permission to put him to death for treason. Darien laughed at the idea. He said it was better to be put to death for treason than to become a slave to the Palatians.

"The king was amazed at Darien's arrogance. Darien said that the king, of all people, should know that the Unseen One would protect them and give them victory. The king called him a fanatic and said that if he was so confident about the Unseen One, maybe he should go out and do something about the Palatians himself. Darien took the dare and said that he would.

"The whole army watched with their mouths hanging open as Darien headed straight across the battlefield. He didn't have on a uniform, he didn't take a pistol or a rifle— he didn't have any protection at all." The fair-haired boy stopped for a moment. By now, every boy in the car had put down his work and was listening.

"Commander Soren was told by his soldiers that a boy from Marus was walking across the field. Soren was angry. He expected King Lawrence to come himself to surrender. 'He sent me a boy?' Soren yelled. 'Give me my rifle. I'll send that boy back with a message—as a corpse.' Soren took his rifle and headed across the field toward Darien.

"They got closer and closer to each other. Soren started to curse at Darien. Darien didn't flinch. Then, still walking, Soren lifted up his rifle and took aim at Darien. Darien didn't lose a step. He kept on going. Soren laughed and started to squeeze the trigger. Darien yelled, 'To the glory of the Unseen One!' and that made Soren angry.

" 'I won't shoot this pup,' Soren said and threw down his rifle. He pulled his sword from its sheath. 'I'll send him back to King Lawrence in pieces!' Meanwhile, Darien kept walking toward Soren, who raised his sword. When he was just a few feet from Soren, Darien pulled out a pocketknife—the one he whittles with. It's a little thing; maybe he'll show it to you sometime. Anyway, with a flick of his wrist, Darien threw that little knife at Soren. It hit him right in the heart. My father was there, and he saw the whole thing. It hit Soren in the heart, and he died right where he stood.

"Did Darien stop and turn back? No. Darien kept right

on walking, went up to the commander's dead body, grabbed his rifle, and started firing like a madman at the Palatians. Everyone was so shocked that they didn't have time to think. The Palatians started to run, and King Lawrence, seeing the opportunity, yelled for his men to attack. They did, and they beat the Palatians back to the border."

"That's amazing," Kyle said, wide-eyed.

The fair-haired boy nodded. "Since then, he's become one of our greatest generals. Ever. The whole country loves him."

"And it all started with just a pocketknife?"

"A pocketknife and the power of the Unseen One," another boy said.

Kyle cocked an eyebrow. "So who is this Unseen One that everybody keeps talking about?"

"Not everybody talks about the Unseen One," the fair-haired boy answered. "We do because we believe. But once you get off this train, you won't find very many people who believe anymore."

"But what is the Unseen One?" Kyle asked.

The fair-haired boy opened his mouth to speak, but a bell suddenly rang. "The officers want us," he said, and, quick as rabbits, the boys jumped up and raced out of the train car.

Her wrists tied with a thick rope, Anna was led by Titus like a dog on a leash. From the palace, they weaved their way through litter-strewn alleys and passages until they emerged in a large market area. At the edge, Titus untied Anna but instantly grabbed her arm in his big hand. "You'll behave or suffer the consequences," he said.

She winced at the dazzling sunlight and felt as if her eyes were being assaulted by brighter colors than she'd ever seen before. Titus led her past booths and stalls filled with fruit, vegetables, meat, newspapers, household items, and even live animals. Men in smocks and women in aprons busied themselves with their work, while some chatted idly about the weather and the state of the economy. All had a look and clothes that reminded Anna of pictures she'd seen in her history books of the Civil War. The market smelled of animals and earth, with an occasional hint of freshly baked bread.

Anna hadn't eaten or slept all night. Though no rats had come to nibble on her, she hadn't wanted to take the chance that they might. She had spent the entire night awake and hoping she'd snap out of this awful dream.

She pleaded with Titus whenever she had the chance. She told him again and again that he was making a big mistake and

even threatened him with what her parents would do if they
found out he was treating her so badly. He told her repeatedly
to shut up or he'd belt her. But he did let go of her arm.

Halfway across the market, Anna tripped and fell into a
puddle of mud. That made Titus angry, and he began to kick
at her to get up. She easily dodged the thrusts of his short,
stumpy legs. That made him even angrier.

"Get up!" He kicked out harder and harder. She quickly
evaded him. He thrust out his leg in the hardest kick of all,
lost his balance, and fell into the mud with a large *splat*. If the
situation weren't so serious, Anna might have giggled over
how silly the two of them must have looked. A crowd had
gathered and did what Anna dare not: They laughed.

"You're going to get yours!" Titus spat, his face beet red.

Before she could get out of reach, he roughly grabbed her
arm. He climbed to his feet, not caring whether he twisted
her arm this way or that to do it, and yanked her up. "I'm not
sure what your value will be once I thrash you for this," he
growled, "but I don't care anymore!"

"Help me!" Anna called out to the crowd on the gamble
that they might respond. "He's going to make me a slave!"

The crowd immediately went about their business as if
nothing had happened—or was about to happen—to the
poor girl. Anna felt the sting of despair as Titus jerked her
out of the mud.

"What goes on, Titus?" inquired a low, gravelly voice.

Titus swung around to see who spoke. "What?" he said.

An old man stepped around from behind a vegetable
booth. He had a slender, pale face with wild, white hair and
a thin beard and mustache. He wore a long, black overcoat
that seemed to droop from his skeletal body. Underneath,
Anna noticed that he wore a collarless shirt, waistcoat, and

old-fashioned breeches, stockings, and shoes—like the people who had lived during the American Revolution. It was an odd contrast to the way everyone else was dressed.

"I want to know what you are doing," the old man said.

Anna heard Titus's sharp intake of breath. He recognized the old man. "You're here!" Titus said. "I thought you were . . ."

"Dead?"

"No, no, of course not. The entire nation would know about that. I just thought that you were . . . were ill."

"Too ill to come visit our lovely capital?"

"I thought you and the king . . . had an understanding."

"The king and I have an understanding. But it's probably not the same understanding. However, there is one thing I do understand: Slavery was outlawed in Marus years ago. Before you were born. How do I know? Because I was the one who outlawed it. Now let the girl go."

Titus tried to sound tough. "I obey the king and his officers. You have no authority over me."

"Don't I?" the old man asked as he took a step forward. Titus stepped back, his grip loosening on Anna's arm.

"No," Titus said, less sure of himself.

"Let me tell you a little something about authority," the old man said with a smile. "It is given, not taken. My authority comes from the Unseen One. From where do the king and his officers get their authority?"

"From . . . from . . ." Titus stammered, but he never found an answer.

The old man held up a finger. "A man your size shouldn't wrestle around in the mud with small children. It's not healthy. Your heart might not be up to it. Perhaps you should have a rest."

Titus suddenly gasped, then collapsed back into the mud. His eyes rolled up in their sockets, then closed, and his massive form relaxed.

Anna quickly moved away from him. "What happened?" she asked. "Is he all right?"

"He's having a little nap," the old man responded. "He'll wake up sooner or later." The old man stooped to look Anna full in the face. "Tell me your story, young lady. You're not from around here, are you?"

"No, sir."

"You're not even from this country, am I correct?"

"Yes, sir. You're correct."

The old man gazed at her thoughtfully. "You're not safe here. I suggest you come with me."

"But . . . why? Who are you?"

The man smiled again. "I am the Old Judge."

The name meant nothing to Anna, but he had saved her, and that was reason enough to go with him. As she and the Old Judge walked past staring eyes in the marketplace, a train whistle blew in the distance.

"That will be the king," the Old Judge said.

"The king is leaving?" Anna asked.

"No, he's just arriving."

Anna was confused. She had seen the king in the palace the day before. Had he left and was now coming back?

"I'm talking about the *real* king," the Old Judge said, sensing Anna's confusion. "The chosen."

Watching from the train window, Kyle was amazed by the large number of people who had crowded onto the station platform to greet General Darien and his men. They cheered loudly as the train hissed and screeched its way to a stop. A delegation of men dressed in brightly colored military uniforms and hats emerged from the crowd. They looked serious and formal as they waited for General Darien to step from the train.

A train-car door swung open, and Colonel Oliver climbed onto the platform. He was followed by several other officers from General Darien's regiment. The crowd grew silent as they watched. Then General Darien appeared in the doorway. The crowd went wild with cheers, flag-waving, and applause. General Darien blushed, then smiled and waved. The delegation stepped forward the second Darien's feet touched the platform. A young man in uniform with wavy dark hair and a thin mustache broke ranks and unceremoniously embraced Darien.

"Darien!" he cried out happily.

"Hello, George," Darien said with a laugh as they thumped each other on the back with all the affection of close brothers. A military band struck up a tune Kyle had never heard before.

"Sorry about all the fuss, but word got around that you'd made it back safely, and, well . . ." The one called George gestured at the crowds, the soldiers, and the band. "I'm afraid we'll have to return to the palace with a lot of pomp and circumstance."

General Darien nodded. "Then let's get on with it. What about my men?"

"We have cars for them to follow in," George said. "There'll be a brief reception in the Great Hall, and then we'll let you all get some much-needed rest."

Kyle joined the rest of Darien's men in large, old-fashioned touring cars. The tops were pushed back so that everyone could wave at the throngs who lined the streets leading to the palace.

Kyle had never seen such a display of affection for a public figure. Nor had he ever seen a city as grand as Sarum. Wide avenues of beautiful green trees and manicured lawns stretched out to majestic buildings of brick, stone, and marble. Some had broad stairs leading up to magnificent porticos and colonnades and the biggest windows Kyle had ever laid eyes on. The avenues spilled onto circles and squares containing monuments and statues acknowledging people and places Kyle had never heard of. Once again he was struck by how vibrant the colors were.

As the parade of cars pulled to the front entrance of the king's palace, Kyle looked to the left and the right. Both wings of the royal residence disappeared into a forest and rounded off in a way that looked as if they went on forever. The main building was adorned with a golden rotunda with a statue of an angel on top.

The king's servants met the entourage and led them through an arched door into an ornate foyer filled with paintings, statues, and a wide marble staircase. Kyle imagined that a tank could drive up those stairs without any trouble. They detoured down a grand hallway lined with more paintings, alcoves with statues, gold-leaf borders, and lamps hanging from carved pilasters.

Finally, they swung off through a double doorway into the Great Hall. It was great indeed, with high walls of carved wood, cornices, ornately framed portraits and mirrors, and tall, triangular windows that seemed to point to an elaborately painted ceiling filled with frescoes of muscular men engaged in battles of all descriptions. The room looked as if it could accommodate hundreds of people without anyone feeling cramped.

Kyle sat with the rest of the troops in chairs facing a stage with wingback chairs and a lavishly designed podium.

Kyle suspected by the way the other members of the audience were dressed that the room was filled with dignitaries and officers from other parts of the country. The king—there was no mistaking him with that crown on his head—took the podium and welcomed the soldiers home from their daring adventures. The audience applauded.

The king continued, "It is with great pride that we honor you today. Your escapades have been the talk of all the nations. Our enemies now know that nothing is beyond the abilities of General Darien and his fighting forces!"

At this, General Darien's men shouted and clapped.

The king waved his arms for the men to quiet down. Then he continued, "General Darien, I believe you have a presentation to make?"

General Darien strode across the stage to another round of applause. When he had reached the podium, he began, "Sire, fellow officers of the royal army, ladies and gentlemen, I am proud to stand here before you today." He smiled wryly. "I'm proud to stand *anywhere,* in fact. We had some close calls in our encounters with the Palatian officers." Everyone laughed.

Darien went on, "As you know, I'm little more than a farm boy who has been blessed beyond his dreams. When the king said he would allow me to marry one of his daughters, I felt humbled and unworthy. It seemed that the only way to accept his graciousness was to do something to prove myself. Most of you know that I agreed to bring back the medals of 100 Palatian officers." He gestured to Colonel Oliver. The colonel and another soldier carried a box forward and placed it on the stage. "Your highness, I'm pleased to report that I have brought you the medals of 200 Palatian officers!"

Pandemonium broke out as the crowd leaped to its feet. The people began to chant, "Darien! Darien! Darien!" over and over. Kyle watched with fascination. He thought for a moment that General Darien could have told these people to do anything—anything at all—and they would have done it. But their admiration wasn't shared on the stage. Kyle couldn't help but notice that the king looked sour-faced, as did many of the officers with him. Was it possible that the king wasn't happy with Darien's success?

When the noise died down, Darien concluded by saying, "Sire, these are only tokens. But I believe they symbolize the power and determination of your people to serve you at home and abroad, in the luxury of peace or in fields of war. May your name bring joy to our allies and strike fear in the hearts of our enemies!" The crowd applauded enthusiastically again as Darien stepped away from the podium.

The king's face worked from a frown into a forced smile. He said, "Thank you, General Darien. Two hundred medals? I'm sorry, but our laws don't allow for you to marry two of my daughters!" The people laughed as he went on, "You do us a great honor, General. And it gives me added pleasure to announce my permission for you to marry my daughter Michelle, in the Sarum Cathedral, *next Saturday.*"

Wild applause followed once more. A beautiful young woman with long chestnut hair and large eyes that darted around nervously appeared in the wings of the stage and was led to General Darien. The king clasped their hands together. Kyle assumed it was Michelle. The king raised his arms, and the people got to their feet again with shouts, chants, stomping feet, and clapping hands. The roar of the ocean could not have been heard in that hall, Kyle thought.

But Kyle couldn't take his eyes off the king. For all the bravado and praise, Kyle thought that he looked like a very unhappy man.

CHAPTER

5

The Old Judge helped Anna into his horse-drawn wagon. He gave her some fruit to eat and then told her to rest while they drove to his cottage in the small village of Hailsham, several miles from the capital. Resting was easy; it was a glorious summer's day. Anna stretched out to greet the warmth of the sun, which somehow seemed bigger here, and let it soak into her body. She still hadn't gotten over the dampness of the dungeon. She dozed for a while and only woke up when the wagon wheel bumped a large rock on the unpaved road.

Anna yawned and looked around. Shafts of light shone on the green hills and groves of trees and highlighted the village of Hailsham, which, as she now saw, sat in the center of a valley. It was composed mostly of a small cluster of shops and offices and a few cottages sprinkled around the outskirts. Nearby, the railroad track cut like a scar into one of the hillsides. Somehow it didn't take away from the beauty, though. The whole scene looked to Anna like the kind of village you'd find on a picture postcard of New England.

The Old Judge's cottage sat between a field and a forest. It was a simple building, mostly white except for dark beams of timber that ran from the thatched roof to the ground. The leaded windows were shuttered and had window boxes filled with flowers of all kinds. Roses, carnations, pansies—Anna couldn't name them all. When Anna and the Old Judge had climbed out of the wagon, he lifted the latch on the heavy brown door and invited her in.

The main room had dark paneling, a fireplace, and two comfortable-looking chairs sitting on a colorful carpet. Off to one side were a large hutch and several bookcases filled with books of all kinds. A grandfather clock watched them indifferently, its arm swinging from left to right and back again.

A second room served as the kitchen, with a stove, sink, and open cupboards containing a modest array of dishes and food containers. Anna noted three doors leading to what she guessed were the bedrooms. The main room was naturally cool since the trees from the forest blocked the sun when it was at its highest point. She sighed contentedly. It might have been the most charming place she'd ever seen in her young life.

"After I take care of the horses and wagon, I'll make us some tea, and then we'll have a little chat," the Old Judge said. He went to put the wagon in his small barn and unhitch the horses to run in the field.

Anna sat down in one of the chairs and glanced at the clock. It was 3:02. Without meaning to, she fell asleep again. When she awoke, a small fire was crackling in the fireplace, and the Old Judge was reading a book in the chair across from her. "I'm sorry," Anna said sleepily. "Did I sleep long?"

The Old Judge closed his book and peered at her over his reading glasses. "Not long," he said.

She glanced at the grandfather clock. It said it was 5:17. "Oh," she said, sorry to have slept for more than two hours.

The Old Judge pointed to a cup and saucer and plate on the end table next to her. "I made you a fresh cup of tea," he explained, "and there are some pastries for you to munch on."

She thanked him and devoured the pastries. She had forgotten how hungry she was. When she finished eating, she still felt hungry and wondered when dinner would be.

"Would you like more?" the Old Judge asked. "Are you still hungry?"

Her parents had taught her that asking for more was rude, whether one was hungry or not. "I'm okay, thank you," she said.

"I don't think you're being honest with me," the old man said. "You're still hungry or *those* wouldn't be there." He tilted his head toward the end table.

Anna looked over and barely stifled her surprise. The empty plate now had several more pastries on it. She looked around to see if the Old Judge had a servant waiting on them. The cottage was empty, however, except for the two of them. She rubbed her eyes and thought, *I must be very, very tired. Or am I still dreaming?*

The Old Judge watched her with a fixed smile as she ate two more pastries. "Is that better?" he asked.

"Yes, sir," she replied. Her hunger was taken care of, for the moment. She reached over to the end table for her cup of tea and was startled yet again. The plate of pastries was empty. *But I only had two, and there must've been seven or eight on the plate,* she nearly said out loud. She bit her tongue, however, and didn't say a word. She thought she *must* be dreaming.

"Let's talk about your situation," the old man said.

"My situation?" she asked.

"Tell me why you're here."

"I don't know why I'm here," she answered. "I don't even know how I got here."

"You've been chosen for something. You don't know what it is?"

"No, sir. All I know is that one minute I was in an abandoned house in the middle of the woods in Odyssey, and the next minute I was in the king's closet."

The Old Judge took off his glasses. "That's very interesting."

Surprised, Anna asked, "You believe me?"

"Why wouldn't I?"

"Nobody else has."

"We're surrounded by men of little imagination and no faith," the Old Judge said wearily.

"I'm not sure that *I'd* believe me," Anna confessed.

"Do you believe you?"

"Yes."

"Then I believe you too."

Anna was genuinely puzzled. "But . . . *why* do you believe me?"

"Because the ancient ways of the Unseen One are full of mystery. Just because your 'Odyssey' can't be found on any of our maps doesn't mean it isn't real. Obviously *you're* real, so there must be something to your story. And I know that the Unseen One is real, so there you are."

"There I am? *Where* am I?" Anna asked.

"In the middle of a wonderful mystery!" the Old Judge exclaimed. "Now, drink your tea."

"I think it's gotten cold," Anna said.

"Is it?" he asked as he put his glasses back on.

Anna reached over for the teacup. It was filled to the brim and steaming hot.

"That's strange," she said.

"What is?" the Old Judge asked. His voice was farther away than it had been. He now stood in the doorway to the kitchen, a tray in his hand containing two cups of tea. She shook her head. He'd been sitting in the chair a moment ago.

How did he move so fast?

"I must be dreaming," she said. She looked at the grand-father clock. It now said it was 3:06.

The Old Judge smiled at her. For the first time, she noticed that his eyes were different colors. One was blue, the other green. "Were you dreaming, or are you dreaming now?" he asked.

The celebration banquet in the Great Hall ended, and Darien released his men to go home to their families. Kyle waited, unsure of what to do or where to go. He worried that Darien had forgotten him now that they were back in the capital. But Darien hadn't. He insisted that Kyle return home with him until they could figure out what to do next.

Darien lived in a manor that the king had given him after he'd defeated the Monrovians in a long, grueling battle. Built in a Gothic style with pointed arches, ornate stonework, and elaborate gables, the manor was on the outskirts of the city, nestled in a cozy corner of the royal forest. It wasn't as large as it was complicated, with halls and rooms twisting and turning in different directions.

"It has more rooms than I ever expect to use in my lifetime," Darien explained to Kyle. "I don't bother with the east wing of the house. The west wing suits me perfectly." That wing had a kitchen, dining room, library, and four bedrooms. They established that Kyle would sleep in the room that overlooked the garden. It didn't matter much to Kyle where he slept. He was more worried about his sister and his family. By now he'd been gone for more than a day. Everyone at home would be alarmed. Maybe even the police were searching for him.

In the library, Darien sat down at a grand piano and began to play a tune that, to Kyle, sounded classical. A maid interrupted to take instructions from Darien for their dinner. He simply said to fix him his "favorite." Kyle wandered over to a tall suit of armor with a colorful shield and a long sword clasped to its side. He could see his reflection in the shiny chest plate.

"We'll rest tonight," Darien said as he played. "Tomorrow I'll take you to see the Old Judge."

Just then, someone tapped on the glass of the double doors that led into the garden. It startled Kyle, but Darien acted as if he'd expected the noise. He got up from the piano, parted the curtains, and opened one of the doors. Prince George stepped in. The two men shook hands and clapped each other on the back and said the kinds of things men say when they haven't seen each other in a long time.

Then Prince George saw Kyle and smiled. "So this is the boy who saved your life," he said.

"He is indeed," Darien replied. "Kyle, this is our beloved Prince George, the son of the king and my greatest friend."

"Hi, Your Honor—er, Highness—er, *sire.*" Kyle blushed as Prince George laughed.

"Our servant Damaris is fixing dinner. Are you hungry?" Darien asked George.

George shook his head. "I can't stay long. My father is expecting me for some state function tonight. But I wanted to talk to you about something urgent." He darted an uneasy glance at Kyle as if to ask, "Can he be trusted?"

Darien nodded. "Say what you must. We are all trusted friends here. Aren't we, Kyle?"

Kyle replied, "Yes, sir. I'm in big trouble otherwise."

The two men laughed, then sat down on a thick red

sofa next to the dormant fireplace. Prince George's face grew earnest.

"I'm here to warn you," he said. "The king is in a dangerous frame of mind. I'm not sure what has seized his disposition, but it's something dark and threatening."

"Are you in any sort of danger?" Darien asked.

Prince George sighed. "I'm not, but you may be."

"Me?" Darien's face lit up with surprise. "I've done nothing against the king. I've served him well, I thought."

"You've served him *too* well. Your successes make him think he's a failure. Your popularity makes him feel unappreciated. Your acceptance makes him feel rejected."

"But he's the *king*," Darien said.

Prince George nodded. "He's the king, yes, but he feels that his position is threatened. He imagines that you may be maneuvering your way to become the next king."

"He is my king as long as he lives!" Darien exclaimed. "I would do nothing to take his throne away from him . . . or you."

Prince George stood up and paced thoughtfully. "There's no point in fooling ourselves," he said after a moment. "I will never be king. You are the chosen one. You will reign one day. The Old Judge said so."

Darien implored, "He said I was chosen, but never for what or even for *when*. Stop this nonsense, George. I'm a loyal subject of the king, your father. I would not lift a finger against him."

"I know that, Darien. But my father doesn't."

"He used to. He has treated me like a son. Would I spit on that? Would I shove a dagger in the back of a man who treated me so well?"

Prince George moved closer to his friend. "My father isn't

himself these days. You know he hasn't been the same since his last argument with the Old Judge. He's fearful and suspicious. I don't know what they said to each other, but it's changed my father. That's why I'm here to warn you."

The two men gazed at each other silently for a moment.

"Thank you, George," Darien said softly.

"Surround yourself with only those you trust whole-heartedly. My father has eyes and ears everywhere." George crossed the room to the double doors and opened one. The smells of the flowers in the garden wafted in. Halfway through the door, he turned back and said, "And, Darien . . ."

Darien faced his friend.

"When you do become king, remember me." Then he was gone.

Darien was in a thoughtful mood for the rest of the evening. He didn't eat much of his dinner, which annoyed Damaris because she'd fixed his favorite meal of lamb, potatoes, carrots, and a breadlike pastry that Kyle didn't recognize. Kyle thought the food was delicious and wolfed it down as politely as he could.

Just as Damaris was clearing away their plates, a messenger arrived from General Liddell. He was a young man dressed in a smart, gray uniform. After a quick salute, he said, "A renegade group from Adria has crossed the border and attacked a town in the Territory of Peace. General Liddell wants you to join him and his brigade in driving the Adrians back into their own land."

"Tell the general that my men are in no condition to fight so soon after their return," said Darien.

"General Liddell anticipated your concern," the messenger said. "The general doesn't want your men. Just you."

Darien considered this for a moment, then nodded.

"All right. Tell the general I'll come."

The messenger saluted again and, with a click of his heels, turned and left.

"What's your pleasure, Kyle?" Darien asked when they were alone again.

"My pleasure?"

"You can stay here until I return, or you can go with me as my personal assistant."

Kyle was surprised. "You want *me* to go into a battle with you?"

"I doubt it'll be much of a battle. A small skirmish mostly." Darien leaned back in his chair. "It'll mean a delay in our speaking with the Old Judge about getting you home."

Kyle considered it for a moment. He could rush back to his worrying sister and grandparents or get to see a real battle. If only he could send a message somehow! But he couldn't. So what should he do? "I'll go with you," he said finally.

Darien smiled. "I thought you might."

The battle—if that's what it could be called—took place in the town of Krawley, some two miles inside the Territory of Peace. In theory, the Territory of Peace was a neutral zone between Marus and Adria, established 100 years before in the Treaty of the Kings. "But the Adrians are barbarians at heart," Darien explained to Kyle on the train the next morning. "Seven years ago, they slaughtered their king and his entire family. Now they're a loose collection of rebel factions who are trying to take over the entire country. Every once in a while, they decide to venture into our realm just to stir things up. It's annoying mostly."

"It seems like you're surrounded by people who like to attack your country," Kyle observed. "The Palatians, the Adrians . . . Is everybody out to get you?"

Darien chuckled and nodded. "I think they are. Ours is a beautiful and blessed country. Our rival nations believe that if they can conquer us, they'll share in what we have. But they don't understand that it's the *people* who make a nation great, not the land. If you conquer us, you'll conquer the very thing that makes Marus worth having. It's like caging a bird for its song. Once caged, the bird will stop singing."

When Kyle and Darien went to meet with General Liddell

in his private car, Kyle noticed that the general was a stern-looking man with distinctive features: primarily a handlebar mustache and a scar on his cheek. He ignored Kyle—even though Darien introduced them—and got down to business with Darien about how to attack the Adrians. Kyle sat quietly in the corner while General Liddell, Darien, and several other officers made their plans.

In Lester, a town a few miles from Krawley, the train stopped and unloaded Liddell's soldiers, artillery, horses, and provisions. The local garrison met them and, together, they numbered almost 1,000. "Can you ride a horse?" Darien asked Kyle.

Kyle had to confess that he couldn't.

"Then you'll ride with me," Darien said. On horseback, they joined the cavalry and rode toward Krawley.

The battle for Krawley was nothing like what Kyle had imagined. He thought there would be a lot of shooting and hand-to-hand combat. There wasn't. For one thing, they found that the Adrians had retreated from the town itself and were now hiding in the nearby hills. For another thing, Marutian cannons on large wheels were rolled in to drive the Adrians out. They fired shells at the hills mercilessly for an entire morning. The constant *boom, boom, boom* gave Kyle a headache.

When the Adrians stopped firing back, the Marutian army marched into the hills to see if the Adrians had deserted or were prepared to surrender. Kyle again rode with General Darien on his horse. Once in the hills, they found evidence that the Adrians had indeed been there. A few bodies littered the camps and rocky inclines where the shells had hit with the most force. Kyle got physically sick at the sight. They were men. And they were dead. It was awful.

He retched behind one of the gun carriages.

Darien patted him lightly on the back and handed him a canteen full of water. "It doesn't get better," he whispered.

"Spread out and search for prisoners," General Liddell ordered. As second only to the king, General Liddell could command Darien like no other officer. "You check those rocks to the north," he told Darien.

"They've retreated, I'm sure," Darien said.

"Check anyway," General Liddell insisted.

With a handful of men, Darien and Kyle went up into the northern part of the hills.

"They'd be fools to stay after that shelling," Darien told Kyle as they sat down on a large rock a few minutes later. They shared water from a stream.

"General Liddell was pretty sure he wanted you to look around, though," Kyle said.

"So he was."

Kyle glanced at the soldiers canvassing the area. From a distance, they looked like wild animals grazing in the grassy knolls. A flicker of light from farther above them caught Kyle's eye. He squinted as an odd feeling settled in the pit of his stomach. A man was leaning against a rock with a rifle pointed in their direction. *How strange,* Kyle thought, the feeling in his stomach making him nauseated.

Then he realized what the man was doing. Kyle leaped up and threw himself at General Darien. They both tumbled off the rock to the ground as splinters of gravel sprayed upward from a bullet that had just missed them. A fraction of a second later, they heard the sharp report of the gunfire echo around them. A great commotion broke out among the soldiers. Some knew instantly what had happened and fired in the direction of the man. Others rushed to make sure General Darien hadn't been hit.

What they found was the bizarre sight of their general with his back on the ground and Kyle lying on top of him.

"Are you all right?" Kyle asked as he rolled off of Darien.

"You have more strength than I would've given you credit for," Darien replied pleasantly. He called out to his second-in-command, "Bryson! Bryson!"

Colonel Bryson came around the rock, his face panicked. "Are you all right, sir? Have you been hit?"

"No," Darien said. "Thanks to my guardian angel. Was it an Adrian assassin?"

"We don't know yet, sir." Colonel Bryson disappeared from view again. More shots were fired, then someone yelled, "Over here!"

Darien leaned against the rock. "What am I going to do with you?" he asked Kyle. "This is the second time you've saved my life. I'm in your debt and deeply grateful to you." He shook Kyle's hand vigorously. "If I were a king, I'd knight you . . . thank you."

"You're welcome," Kyle said, turning a deep crimson.

They stood up, careful to stay behind the cover of the rock, and dusted themselves off. "I'm hesitant now to ever let you go back to Odyssey. No doubt I'll be killed the instant you go."

Colonel Bryson returned just then and said, "We got him, sir."

"Is he alive?"

"I'm afraid not." Colonel Bryson shuffled awkwardly for a moment.

"Well?"

"He's one of ours."

"What do you mean?"

"He's not an Adrian. He's one of our soldiers, though I don't know with whom he serves."

"One of our own men tried to kill me?" Darien asked, perplexed.

"It would appear so, sir."

Darien tapped his chin thoughtfully. "Now why would he want to do a thing like that?"

A few minutes later, when they had explained the incident to General Liddell, he promised to conduct a full-blown investigation into the murder attempt. A look in his eye, however, made Kyle think the case would never be solved.

Three days passed. While Kyle chased the Adrians and then returned to Sarum with Darien, Anna stayed with the Old Judge at his cottage. She mended her clothes with a thread and needle the Old Judge had given her, walked through the lush green forest and over the small hills, and, at night, stared with an insatiable curiosity at the two moons.

Part of their routine—one that Anna suspected the Old Judge had been doing for years—was to begin the day with prayer to the Unseen One and reading from the Sacred Scroll. Since Anna didn't know much about either, the Old Judge used the time to teach her.

"The Unseen One is the Creator and Sustainer of all things," he explained. "He is everywhere at all times; all-seeing, all-knowing, all-powerful."

"Like our God," Anna said, relating the description to what she knew from her world.

"Not *like* God," the Old Judge corrected. "The Unseen One *is* God. The God of love and justice."

Anna pointed to the large roll of paper spread out in front of them. "Is that your Bible?"

He pondered her question. "The word *bible* means 'book.' In which case, the Sacred Scroll might be considered that. It contains an account of the relationship between the Unseen One and the created. It spans history back to the beginning of time. It tells the story of the faithful and the faithless, of despots and statesmen, of common folk and warriors, of heroes and cowards. I'm writing sections of it now myself, recounting my own work as a chosen voice for the Unseen One."

"Chosen? You keep using that word. What does it mean?"

"It means several things. We are chosen because of the Unseen One's love for us. That love reaches out to us, and we, in turn, respond to it by faith—by our belief in the Unseen One."

Anna nodded. That much she could understand.

The Old Judge continued, "Yet we, the faithful, are also chosen in specific ways, to do specific tasks for the Unseen One. I was chosen before I was born."

"Before you were born?" Anna said, surprised. "Then how did you know you were chosen?"

"My parents had dedicated me to the Unseen One at my birth. I was a child when they gave me over to the priests to be trained."

"Your parents gave you away?"

"They knew I was chosen—or called—by the Unseen One. It was their duty to give me to those who would help me hear that call more clearly. We had many priests in those days. Very few are left."

Anna was still thinking about the Old Judge's being separated from his parents. "Didn't you miss them?" she asked.

"I still saw them. We visited often. But I would not have refused the Unseen One's call even if I could."

Anna knitted her brow. "But . . . how did your parents . . . or *you* know you were called?"

"That's part of the mystery, I suppose," he said. "My mother knew from the moment I was conceived. I inherited that knowledge from her. Others are called later in life."

"How do *they* know?"

The Old Judge patted his beard thoughtfully. "It is a matter of faith, child, and it works differently from person to person. My parents had faith in the Unseen One, and their faith extended to me—that is, until I had faith of my own to believe."

Anna still didn't understand. "So which part comes first? Your faith or being chosen?"

"That's like asking whether the sun first rises or the sun first sets." The Old Judge smiled. "All things begin with the Unseen One. We could not have faith unless the Unseen One first gave us the capacity for faith. We believe because He makes it possible to believe. Once we believe, then it's safe to assume we are chosen. Chosen for *what* is part of the mystery. But know this: Where there is faith, there is calling."

Anna shook her head. It was too much to take in. "But *how* do you know what the calling is?"

"Sometimes the knowledge comes in visible and tangible ways. For most, though, it comes through prayer and the study of the Sacred Scroll. In time, the voice is unmistakable. The calling is there. Sometimes the knowledge comes through an old prophet like myself. I identify the one who has been called, even before they know it themselves. As I did to make Lawrence the king. And as I did to make General Darien the king."

"Lawrence and Darien—both kings?" Anna asked. "You called both? But won't that cause a lot of trouble?"

"It certainly will," the Old Judge said sadly. "But the trouble is not from the Unseen One. The problems come when a man is disobedient to the call—allows himself to be seduced by man-made powers and forces—and turns his back on the Unseen One. He is leading this nation to faithlessness. So a new king had to be chosen. General Darien is that king."

"I don't think King Lawrence will like that very much."

"It's the way of man to avoid the consequences of his faithlessness. King Lawrence will cling to an imaginary crown for as long as he can and lead the people of Marus even further away from the Unseen One. However, in his heart, Lawrence knows his rule is over. He rejected the Unseen One, and now the Unseen One has rejected him. Does he accept it? No. It drives him to madness even now."

At night, Anna had troubling dreams. They weren't nightmares but dreams that left her feeling disturbed when she awoke in the morning. Twice, the Old Judge came to her in the dreams. "You've been chosen," he said. "But your heart is not ready. In your heart, you must have faith in the Unseen One. Then you will be His voice."

Anna argued, "But nobody ever listens to me. I couldn't even keep my brother from going into that old house."

The Old Judge smiled and said, "A greater power than your brother was at work. You two were brought here to be a voice and a protector."

"A voice and a protector?"

Then he faded away. She woke up.

Other times, in the middle of the day, she would be doing something normal like working in the garden or reading one of the Old Judge's books, and suddenly it was as if she were no longer where she was but had been transported to another place to witness scenes of other people. The scenes made no sense to her. In one instance, she saw King Lawrence throwing a temper tantrum in his study.

"Still alive?" he screamed.

"The assassination attempt in the hills near Krawley failed. The fool missed," reported someone Anna couldn't see.

The king swept his arm across his desk, sending the paper, pens, ink blotter, telephone, and decorations exploding away. Then, suddenly, Anna saw him alone. He wept like a child.

"Please," he prayed with tear-filled eyes, "let me have the kingdom back."

When the prayer didn't bring him satisfaction, he marched around the room angrily, pouting like a spoiled brat. Anna found it a pathetic thing to watch.

Then, just as suddenly, she was back at the cottage, in the same position, doing the same thing she'd been doing before the weird "daydream."

She didn't tell the Old Judge about her dreams. She was afraid he would think she was crazy or hallucinating. Anyway, she knew, adults rarely believed her when she told them unusual things. When she was younger, she had an active imagination, often thinking up other lands and people and stories about them. But when she told her parents or teachers about her imaginings, they just smiled and nodded dismissively. "What an imagination!" they'd say, then tell her to get back to her math homework or science project. As she got older, she stopped imagining so much. It wasn't practical or helpful with her grades at school. "Stick with the *real* world," the adults told her. So she did. But now that the real world had disappeared, she wondered if her imagination had taken over again. For all she knew, this whole experience was just a dream and, in reality, she was lying with a high fever in a bed somewhere.

"When can I go home?" she asked the Old Judge on their third day together.

He shrugged and said, "I wish I could tell you."

"Does that mean you know and can't tell me or that you don't know?"

He gazed at her. His odd-colored eyes captured her. "These things must be taken by faith—one day at a time," he replied. He waited as if he expected her to tell him something. She was tempted to tell him about the dreams but resisted. He sighed. "One day at a time," he said again.

The night before the wedding of Darien and Michelle, King Lawrence threw a small banquet at his palace. The king was there with his entire family, including Prince George; his two brothers, Andrew and William; their sister Mary; and her new husband, Frederick, the prince of Albany. (The king's wife, their mother, had died a couple of years before.) Darien and Michelle were there, of course. Darien's family, who lived on the opposite side of the country, couldn't attend the banquet but were to arrive later that night for the festivities the following day. General Liddell was also there and stayed at the king's elbow the entire evening. There were dozens of servants and attendants as well, including Kyle, who stood off to the side and looked uncomfortable in the formal uniform he'd been made to wear.

The skirmish with the Adrians seemed to dominate most of the discussion that night. General Liddell spoke proudly of his men's skill in battle. Kyle noticed that he didn't refer to Darien by name. In fact, to Kyle's surprise, no one mentioned the attempt to kill Darien at all. At first he thought it was because most people would've considered it rude or bad luck to bring up such a subject on the eve of a wedding. But as Kyle watched the various guests—the king and General Liddell in particular—he had a strong feeling that there were more sinister reasons to keep the subject under wraps. A thought came to him suddenly and for no apparent reason: *The king himself had arranged the murder attempt.* Kyle tried to make the thought go away, but it wouldn't.

Darien and Michelle were attentive to each other. He kissed her hand while she blushed shyly, then gently teased her and treated her playfully as one might treat a friend.

But something was missing. Kyle remembered how his mother and father sometimes looked at each other with a deep affection. Kyle didn't see it in Darien's eyes. Michelle, on the other hand, was nervous and self-conscious. Kyle thought of a girl at school who had developed a crush on him. She had talked to him with ease up until then, but she suddenly became speechless around him. Her feelings got hurt quickly, and she sometimes punched him in the arm for no apparent reason. Michelle reminded Kyle of that girl. It was as if she had a schoolgirl crush on Darien. Was that love? Kyle didn't know for sure.

On the way to the banquet, Darien had briefly explained to Kyle that people often didn't marry for love. They married because their parents had arranged it. Or, in the case of kings and governments, marriages were politically expedient to secure relationships and allies. Kyle had told Darien that he thought those kinds of marriages were sad. "Not always," Darien had said. "Some marriages start out of necessity, then grow into love. Sometimes they begin with basic respect, and that's enough."

Watching Darien and Michelle as the evening went on, Kyle knew they did not love each other. Maybe they shared enough respect to make them happy. Time would tell, he figured.

After dinner had been served, the crowd urged Darien to play a few pieces on the grand piano that stood in the corner of the room. He reluctantly agreed and performed songs that made Kyle want to cry and leap for joy at the same time. They stirred something in his heart in a way that he never thought music could do. The guests were so moved that, when Darien finished the last song, no one stirred or applauded.

King Lawrence downed a gobletful of wine, then clapped his hands. He announced in rather slurred speech that he had some surprises for the happy couple. Two servants brought out beautifully wrapped presents for his daughter. She opened them to discover a necklace, earrings, and a ring that had belonged to her mother. Michelle wept and hugged her father in gratitude. For Darien, King Lawrence had an antique crossbow.

"It works!" he said to Darien as he loaded a small arrow onto the horizontal bow. He put the stock against his shoulder and pulled the string back until the arrow was nestled and cocked in its slot. To everyone's dismay, he pointed the crossbow around the room as if he might fire at whatever— or whomever—struck his fancy.

"Sire," General Liddell said and rested a hand on the king's arm.

The king laughed and put the crossbow onto the banquet table. "Oh, don't be so peevish, General," he said.

Crowds had been gathering outside the palace the entire evening, and now they broke into a familiar chant for Darien. "Darien! Darien! Darien!" they called.

Prince George broke the tension by saying jovially, "I believe the crowd would appreciate an appearance by the bride and bridegroom on the balcony." He stood up and waved for a servant to open the double doors. The roar of the crowd intensified. "Darien! Darien! Darien!"

"Go on, Darien," someone encouraged. "Show the world your bride!"

Darien stood up, took his bride's hand, and led her to the balcony. The rest of the banquet guests joined them.

The sight of Darien and Michelle threw people into a frenzy of cheering and shouts. In return, Darien smiled, waved, then kissed the hand of the bride-to-be. The people shouted more loudly in appreciation.

After several minutes of this, Darien indicated that they should go back in to the banquet. "Let's not bore them," he said pleasantly as they turned back toward the banquet hall.

"Bore them?" Prince William said boisterously. "You could never bore them, Darien. They love you. You can do no wrong as far as they're concerned!"

What happened next happened so quickly that Kyle barely had time to act. He glanced over in time to see the king, who was slumped in his chair, reach toward the crossbow. It didn't look like a purposeful act. He casually placed his hand on the stock of the weapon and rubbed the wood lightly. Kyle felt an odd feeling in the pit of his stomach, a sense that something wasn't right. *Does he mean to shoot Darien?* Kyle wondered. But the king's manner was so careless that Kyle couldn't be sure. Yet that feeling, so like the one he had had on the Krawley hillside, said that Darien was in danger. How could he warn Darien without causing a scene?

Kyle looked over at the glass-paned double doors where Darien, Michelle, and the other guests were returning from the balcony. Michelle entered, with Darien following. The king fiddled with the crossbow. His fingers stretched toward the trigger. Kyle reached into his pocket and pulled out a round brass button shaped like a marble, an extra to the same buttons along his waistcoat and cloak. With a quick flick of his wrist—barely noticeable to anyone around him— he threw the button across the floor toward Darien.

Michelle and the guests continued walking into the hall. Darien, who was crossing in front of the grand piano, had turned to say something to one of the guests when his eye caught sight of the button sliding toward his feet. He bent down to pick it up. Suddenly there was a loud *click* and a hissing sound, followed by the arrow from the crossbow slamming into the upright lid of the piano. The force splintered the wood and sent a discordant note shivering through the instrument. It had missed Darien only by inches and would have hit him if he hadn't stooped down. Kyle breathed a deep sigh of relief.

Some of the guests screamed and pushed back. Darien turned in the direction from which the arrow had come. All eyes followed. The king looked up sullenly from his place at the table, his hand still on the crossbow. He said in a wine-filled voice, "My dear boy, I'm so sorry! I was reaching for the confounded thing and it simply went off. A light touch on the trigger. I do apologize. Good thing I wasn't aiming, eh?"

Darien glared at the king without speaking.

"Father!" Michelle cried out.

Prince George strode to the table and snatched up the crossbow indignantly. "You could have killed him!" he growled. He turned quickly. "General Liddell!" he barked.

"Yes, sir." General Liddell broke from the crowd and stepped forward.

"My father has had too much to drink. See him to his room, if you please."

"Yes, sir." General Liddell rounded the table and helped the king to his feet.

"It was an accident!" the king protested drunkenly as General Liddell led him away. "Do you honestly think I'd try to kill my greatest general—the greatest in the entire land? The greatest in history?"

After the king had gone, Darien turned to Michelle, kissed her hand once again, and said, "I will see you tomorrow, my princess." He signaled Kyle, and together they walked toward the door.

"So soon? So early?" Prince Andrew called out. "Now that Father's gone, this party can *really* heat up. Do stay, Darien."

"I'm sorry, but I must think of tomorrow," he said from the door. He gave them a half-salute and walked out, closing the door behind him.

"That was a close call," Kyle said as they walked down the hall.

"Too close, as far as I'm concerned," Darien replied. He handed the button back to Kyle. "This is yours, I assume?"

Kyle nodded.

"Someday you're going to have to explain to me how you always know when my life is in danger."

"I don't know," Kyle said simply as he pocketed the button again. "So Prince George was right. The king wants to kill you."

"It would appear so."

"Unless it really was an accident."

Darien gave Kyle a look of disbelief. "If it was an accident, it would have been an awfully *convenient* accident."

Anna had just finished washing for bed. She grabbed a towel,
dried her face, and looked in the mirror. She gasped. Instead
of seeing her reflection, it was as if she were looking through
a window into a large bedroom with an enormous bed surrounded by thick curtains. At the foot of the bed, King
Lawrence sat with his legs stretched out. General Liddell
pulled at the king's boots. They were in an animated conversation, though Anna couldn't hear it. The king was angry
about something, as usual. Suddenly Prince George stormed
into the room. He shouted at his father. His father shouted
back. Prince George paced, shook his finger at the king as if
rebuking him for something, then left.

More calmly, King Lawrence and General Liddell spoke
to each other. They had the look of two conspirators hatching a dangerous plot. The king was emphatic about what he
wanted done. General Liddell finally saluted and marched
out of the room.

The king staggered to the side of the bed and threw
himself facedown onto the thick cushions. The room was
still for a moment. Then a shadow moved in the window.
The curtains parted, and a woman Anna had never seen
before stepped out. She glanced nervously at the king on
his bed, then crossed the room and leaned against a wall
next to a bookcase. Watching the king closely, she reached
over to the chair rail that lined the wall and pressed something along the top. A secret door in the wall opened, and
she slipped out of the room. The secret door closed, and the

wall looked as solid as it had before.

Anna trembled for a moment, and then the room disappeared, replaced by her face in the mirror. She looked pale. Her knees felt weak, and her arms ached from clutching the washstand tightly. Composing herself, she splashed water on her face again, dried off, and then stepped into the hallway to go to her room.

The Old Judge stood there, waiting for her. "Are you well?" he asked.

Anna swallowed hard. "Yes, sir, I am," she said.

"You look shaken," he said.

She avoided his gaze as she walked past him. "I'm all right," she affirmed.

But she knew his eyes were on her as she slipped into her room. In bed, she pulled her pillow close. *What are these scenes I keep seeing?* she wondered. *Why am I seeing them?* She eventually closed her eyes for a night of restless sleep.

At home once again, Darien sat down at his piano and played songs that were alternately mournful and passionate. Kyle sat nearby and watched him. Darien's playing wasn't an idle amusement. He was thinking as he played, trying to decide what to do next.

Kyle shifted in his seat nervously. "What are you going to do?" he eventually asked.

"A very good question, lad," Darien said. He stopped playing, closed the lid on the piano, and rested his elbows there.

"If you think the king tried to kill you, you'd be crazy to stick around," Kyle said. "Shouldn't you escape while you can?"

Darien shook his head. "What about the wedding tomorrow?" he asked. "I can't simply disappear in the night without an explanation. What would I say? 'Oh, sorry, but I couldn't marry the princess because the king tried to kill me with a crossbow.' It would be an accusation—my word against the king's."

"What if you just don't show up?"

"Another scandal. How could I insult the princess and her royal family like that? The entire nation would be up in arms."

Just then, they heard a light tapping at the French

doors leading to the garden.

Kyle's face brightened. "I'll bet it's Prince George," he said. "He'll know what to do."

Darien crossed over to the doors but didn't open them. Instead, he stood next to the wall and carefully lifted the curtain for a peek. His face registered surprise, and he quickly opened the doors. Princess Michelle, dressed in a black cloak with a hood, rushed in. Kyle, also surprised, stood up.

"What brings you here, my princess?" Darien asked.

"We haven't much time," the princess said. "They're on their way."

"Who is?" Darien asked.

"General Liddell's guards. They've been instructed to arrest you."

"On what charge?"

"Treason."

"That's insane!"

"Insane or not, it's what my father wants."

Darien fumed. "No one will believe it," he insisted. "How could they prove such a thing?"

"You underestimate my father. He has it all worked out. They're going to claim that the man who tried to assassinate you outside Krawley had learned that you were hatching a plot to overthrow the king. You had him killed to keep him quiet."

"I didn't have him killed! The soldiers there will attest to that."

"What soldiers? *General Liddell's* soldiers?" the princess asked, shocked at Darien's naïveté. "They're duty bound to whatever the general and the king tell them. You must leave—*now.*"

Darien eyed her warily. "You're the king's daughter. Why should I believe you?"

The princess opened her mouth to speak, but tears fell from her eyes instead. "I know my father wanted me to marry you so I'd keep an eye on you for him. And I know you're marrying me only because the king wants you to. No one stopped to ask *my* feelings, though. And the truth is, I love you. I have from the first time I met you."

A sympathetic smile crossed Darien's face, and he took the princess's hands in his and kissed them both. "I'm humbled and undeserving of your love, my princess," he said.

A hard pounding at the front door interrupted their tender moment. Darien, Princess Michelle, and Kyle raced into the hallway just as Edward, the head servant, made his way to the door.

"Wait!" Darien told him. "You have to stall them, Edward. Tell them I'm in bed. Give me time."

Edward's dull expression didn't change as he bowed slightly and answered, "Yes, sir."

The three of them turned and raced up the steps to the second floor and Darien's room.

"What do we do now?" Kyle asked after Darien closed and locked the door.

Darien quickly pulled the covers down to the foot of the bed and then went to the corner of the room, where he grabbed a suit of armor that stood there indifferently. *Do they have suits of armor in every room?* Kyle wondered.

"Help me," Darien said to Kyle. Together they pushed the armor onto the bed. Darien yanked the covers over it. He then dimmed the light in the room so that it genuinely looked as if someone were asleep in the bed. "There," he said. "Sleeping like a baby."

Deep voices shouted in another part of the house. Darien went to the window and threw it open. Satisfied that no one was waiting below, he turned to Kyle and asked, "Are you coming?"

"Where else would I go?" Kyle said.

Darien then turned to Princess Michelle. "It's going to look bad for you," he said sympathetically. "Liddell's men will wonder why you're here. Tell them I threatened to kill you if you didn't help me. Attempted murder won't surprise them if they think I'm a traitor."

Michelle nodded silently.

Darien kissed her. "I suppose our wedding day will have to wait," he said with an ironic smile.

She smiled sadly as a tear slipped down her cheek. "I suppose it will," she agreed.

Heavy footsteps invaded the hall just outside the room. Someone jiggled the handle, then began to break down the door.

"Farewell," Darien said to Michelle. Then he hoisted Kyle out of the window, where he grabbed on to a branch of a nearby tree. Darien started to follow, then stopped. "I've forgotten my pistol and my sword!" he exclaimed. "Where are they?"

"You don't have time!" Michelle said firmly.

Darien frowned, then leaped to the tree. He and Kyle climbed down to the ground and ran off into the night.

In her dreams, Anna saw a woman standing in a bedroom. It wasn't the king's bedroom this time—this room was smaller and more modest—but it was the same woman she had seen before. The room wasn't lit very well, so Anna had a hard time making out the shadows. The woman moved to the bed and sat down. Someone slept under the covers. Whoever it was didn't stir. Anna had the impression that the woman was a nurse taking care of someone ill.

The bedroom door was suddenly thrown open. Several men stood silhouetted in the doorway. They were dressed as soldiers, with guns in hand and swords at their sides. The woman stood up and crossed quickly to the men before they could enter the room fully.

The men stopped, surprised to see the woman there. She gestured in appeal to them and then back to the bed as if to say that they shouldn't disturb the sleeper. One of the men waved his arms anxiously at the woman and also pointed to the bed. The woman responded. Finally the man waved her aside and approached the bed with his sword drawn. He threw back the covers. A suit of armor glimmered in the dim light.

Dreams have no sense of time or place. Just as Anna saw the suit of armor, the scene quickly changed to a dark wood. A man Anna didn't know moved hastily through the trees. He was followed by a boy.

"Kyle!" Anna gasped.

Kyle and the man emerged from the woods and stood for a moment on the crest of a hill. They looked out over a valley that Anna recognized. In the distance, she saw the town of Hailsham. Kyle and the man headed for the town.

Seconds later—or was it minutes or an hour?—Anna was awakened by a knocking sound. She sluggishly crawled from her bed and ventured out to the main room of the Old Judge's cottage. The Old Judge, still fully dressed as if he'd never gone to bed, held a lamp high and opened the door.

"Hello, Darien," he said warmly as the man in Anna's dream stepped in. They clasped hands and shook vigorously. Then the Old Judge said, "And you must be—"

"Kyle!" Anna cried out as she rushed to the door.

Kyle turned to his sister, a stunned expression on his face. She gave him a long, hard hug.

CHAPTER

8

Morning came just as Kyle and Anna finished swapping stories of their time in Marus. They were both amazed at their respective adventures and wondered anew about their reason for being in Marus at all. Anna didn't tell Kyle about her bizarre dreams. Nor did Kyle mention how he'd saved Darien's life three times. They talked instead about the effect their disappearance from Odyssey would have on their family.

"Do you think Grandma and Grandpa are worried?" Anna asked.

"Probably," Kyle said. "Maybe the police are looking for us."

But there was nothing they could do about it. Both were resigned to that fact. What neither of them dared mention, though, was the possibility that they might never get back to their own world. That was a worry they didn't dare put into words.

Meanwhile, in another part of the cottage, Darien told the Old Judge everything that had happened with King Lawrence, including the attempt to kill him with the crossbow and the narrow escape from his bedroom thanks to Princess Michelle's warning.

The Old Judge listened and nodded thoughtfully.

"This was inevitable," he said.

"Was it?" Darien asked.

"You were chosen by the Unseen One. Lawrence knows it but won't accept it. What man would?"

"But the king has nothing to fear from me," Darien said firmly.

"Oh, but his madness tells him he does," the Old Judge said. "He knows you've been chosen to replace him."

"I don't know that. No one ever told me I was chosen to be king."

"Perhaps you won't admit it openly, but you've known in your heart that it is true," the Old Judge said, casting a steely gaze at the young man. "Don't you remember when I secretly went to your father's house? Do you think it was for a cup of tea and a pleasant chat? I was sent there by the Unseen One to find you."

"I remember," Darien said quietly. "You laid your hands on my head and claimed I was chosen for an important purpose."

"To be king."

"And now King Lawrence wants to see that it doesn't happen. Nor will I force it to happen. I will not lift a hand against him. You know I won't." Darien folded his arms resolutely.

The Old Judge smiled like a shrewd negotiator. "We're in the hands of the Unseen One."

"I wish someone would tell me who the Unseen One is," Kyle said as he and Anna walked into the room.

"Your sister will explain it as you walk to the village," the Old Judge stated.

"We're going to the village?" Anna asked.

The Old Judge waved her on. "Yes. Bring me back a newspaper. I'd like to see what the king is saying about the cancellation of the wedding."

The children complied, and on the way to the village, Anna told Kyle what she could about the Unseen One.

"The Unseen One must be God," Kyle said, coming to the same conclusion that Anna had.

"Yeah, but here the Unseen One seems so . . . well, it's like He really does things here."

Kyle thought about it for a moment and then said, "Grandma and Grandpa say God does things in our world, too—but you have to believe in Him in your heart to see what He's up to."

Anna remembered the dream she had where the Old Judge said almost the same thing to her. "You must have faith," he'd said. *Do I have that kind of faith?* she asked herself.

"I get the feeling there aren't a lot of people left who believe in the Unseen One," Kyle said.

"I get the same feeling," Anna agreed. "The Old Judge says that King Lawrence and the rest of the country have come up with some kind of do-it-yourself religion. He says it's man-made and that everyone thinks that things just happen because they happen—sort of like fate with a capital F. But the Old Judge thinks the king believes in it because he can't stand being rejected by the Unseen One. If he pretends the Unseen One doesn't exist, he'll get to be king longer."

They reached the village, and Anna slipped into a corner shop that sold groceries, tobacco, and newspapers. When she returned to the street, she was ashen faced. She handed the newspaper to Kyle.

"Plot to Overthrow King Thwarted!" the headline in the *Sarum Herald* shouted in large, black type. The article went on to say that a plot to overthrow the king had been exposed just in the nick of time. For security reasons, the wedding had been canceled. Though it didn't say so directly, the newspaper hinted that General Darien may have been part of the plot. The royal family was leaving the capital city for a safer place until the extent of the plot could be determined.

"The king didn't waste any time, did he?" Kyle said.

Inside the paper were stock black-and-white photos of the royal family. In the center of one page was a photo of Darien and Michelle on stage in the Great Hall on the day the king announced the wedding. Anna put her hand to her mouth with alarm.

"What's the matter?" Kyle asked.

"Is that really the princess?" she said.

"Yeah."

Anna shook her head and spoke so softly that Kyle had a hard time hearing her as she observed, "Weird things are happening here."

Kyle looked curiously at his sister. "Like what?" he asked.

She led Kyle down Hailsham's main street toward the road that would lead them back to the cottage. When they reached an open field, she said, "I keep having dreams, seeing things."

Kyle sounded annoyed at having to wait so long for that statement. "Everybody sees things in their dreams," he said.

"But these are real things," Anna explained. "I saw the king in his bedroom having an argument with that General Liddell guy. I saw the princess, too. She was in the bedroom spying on them. She escaped through a secret door. And then I saw her in another bedroom."

Kyle said impatiently, "She was in Darien's room. She helped us escape. I told you the story. I think you're getting mixed up."

"No. I saw what happened *after* you escaped from his bedroom."

"That's impossible."

Anna shook her head. "Soldiers came in, and the princess stopped them. There was someone in the bed—or that's what I thought. But the soldiers pulled the covers back, and it wasn't a person. Someone had put a suit of armor in the bed."

Kyle's face went pale. No one had mentioned the suit of armor back at the cottage. There was no way Anna could've known about it. "You dreamed that?" he asked.

"Sort of," Anna said, relieved that Kyle seemed to believe her now. "But it's more like a daydream than a dream. It's like . . ." But the words to describe it escaped her. She couldn't say any more.

"Maybe it's because we're in this country," Kyle offered.

"Maybe it's the Unseen One. The Old Judge said that I've been brought here for a reason. If I was, then you were, too. You came here before I did, remember? We were chosen for a reason."

"What kind of reason?"

Anna shrugged. "The Old Judge said something about us being a voice and a protector. Maybe he meant that *I'm* the voice and you're the protector."

Kyle thought about that for a moment. *Protector.* It made sense—and his face reflected the realization.

"What are you thinking?" Anna asked.

Kyle told his sister about the three times he had saved Darien's life. He concluded, "I get this sick feeling in the pit of my stomach. And then the next thing I know, somebody tries to hurt Darien and I save him."

Anna shuddered. "This is very strange."

"Anna . . ." Kyle hesitated as if he wasn't sure he should say more. But he did. "Do you believe in the Unseen One?"

Anna considered her answer carefully, then said, "There's no other way to explain all the things I've seen with the Old

Judge, or in my dreams, or our being here. So, yes, I believe in the Unseen One."

They walked on silently for a while. The cottage appeared just ahead.

Eventually, Kyle asked, "Do you think the Unseen One is on our side? I mean, if we're here for a reason, will the Unseen One take care of us and get us home again?"

"I hope so," Anna said, then added, "I think so."

Kyle sighed deeply. "I hope you're right."

Back at the cottage, Darien read the newspaper, then threw it across the room. "This is unbelievable!" he snarled.

"Unbelievable? *Predictable* is the better word," the Old Judge said.

"At least they didn't say you were a traitor," Kyle said to be helpful.

Darien frowned. "They didn't say it outright, but they implied it. People will be watching."

"The king will pay me a visit," the Old Judge said. "Of that you can be sure."

"Why?"

"Why not? He'll know that you've come to see me." The Old Judge scratched at his beard. "Frankly, I'm surprised he hasn't tried to sneak up on us already."

Darien shook his head. "He'd send someone to arrest me. He wouldn't come all this way himself."

"All this way? He's just over the hill."

Darien looked at the Old Judge quizzically. "What are you talking about?"

"Think about it, son. If they left Sarum for security reasons, where would they go? The king's country estate— and that's all of two miles from here. It is peaceful and secure. Being so close, the king will not resist coming to me."

"Let him come," Darien said. "I won't be here."

"And where will you be?"

"At the king's country estate," Darien said simply.

"What?" Kyle asked. "Are you nuts? I mean, are you nuts, *sir*?"

"If the royal family is there, that would include George. I want to see him."

"To what end?" the Old Judge asked.

"He's my friend," Darien replied. "I want him to know that these allegations are all lies."

"If he's your friend, he knows it already," said the Old Judge.

"And I want to see if he can speak to the king," Darien continued. "Maybe there's a way to appease him, to make him see that I am not his enemy."

The Old Judge scrutinized Darien's face. "You say that so sincerely," he said. "Do you believe it? Do you believe King Lawrence will ever allow you to return to his court?"

"I want to believe it's possible, even if it's impossible."

The Old Judge placed a hand on Darien's shoulder and said gently, "The wheels are in motion, my son. Nothing can be the way it was."

Darien didn't reply but went to the door and pulled it open. Kyle followed.

"Don't go, Kyle," Anna said as he and Darien walked out. "You'll get caught—or hurt."

Kyle looked back over his shoulder and smiled bravely. "Me get caught?" he said lightly. "I'm in the hands of the Unseen One."

"That doesn't mean the Unseen One won't let you get caught," she said.

But the door closed and they were gone.

The Old Judge was right. Shortly after Darien and Kyle left, a handful of soldiers came to the cottage and demanded to see Darien. The Old Judge said truthfully that he wasn't there. When the soldiers declared that they would search the house, the Old Judge blocked their way, fixed a dark eye on them, and said, "You must find it terribly funny to think that Darien would hide in an old cottage like this."

To Anna's amazement, the soldiers began to laugh. "Yeah, it is funny," the captain said as his laughter turned into side-splitting hysterics. The soldiers guffawed uncontrollably, to the extent that they sank to their knees and rolled on their sides. Some of them doubled over with stomach cramps from laughing so hard, and others couldn't breathe. After a few minutes, the captain begged the Old Judge for mercy.

The Old Judge said, "You desire mercy? Then leave this place and you'll have it."

Between chortles and gasps, the captain commanded his men to withdraw. They helped each other up from the ground and stumbled away, their laughter still echoing through the valley as they went.

Anna looked at the Old Judge with an unspoken question.

"Weak-minded men," the Old Judge said offhandedly. "We'll see how the next batch hold up."

"The next batch?"

Sure enough, two hours later, another company of soldiers arrived. They were a harder-looking bunch than the previous men, with expressions that said they probably hadn't laughed in years. The officer in charge seemed to know the Old Judge. "None of your tricks," he barked. "We want Darien."

"He's not here," the Old Judge said.

"We'll see about that," the officer growled. He directed his men to search the house.

Again the Old Judge stepped forward to block their way to the door. "But it's so sad that a man as respected as Darien should be hunted like an animal," he said. "Don't you find it terribly sad?"

"I don't find it sad at all," the officer said. But his eyes filled with tears anyway.

His men began to sob.

"Stop it!" the officer shouted through his own tears. "Don't you see what's happening? He's tricking us!"

The Old Judge gazed at them innocently. "A trick?" he said. "Since when are laughter and tears part of a trick? They are gifts from the Unseen One."

"Keep your gifts to yourself!" the officer said as he wept. "We have to search this house."

"Am I stopping you?" the Old Judge asked.

By now, the soldiers had fallen to their knees, their faces hidden in their hands, the tears pouring from between their fingers. The officer, strong though he was, eventually succumbed and also dropped to the ground. The weeping and wailing of the men brought tears to Anna's eyes, too.

"I'm afraid I'm all out of tissues," the Old Judge said.

Through heaving sobs, the officer told his men to retreat. "This is humiliating!" was the last thing he cried before they were out of sight.

Within the hour, there came a stern knock at the door. "That would be General Liddell, with King Lawrence not too far behind," the Old Judge said to Anna. He went to welcome them.

General Liddell stood erect in the doorway, his face red

and the scar a sliver of white on his cheek. "The king wants to speak to you," he said formally. He tapped the handle of the pistol he had tucked in his belt. "I wouldn't do anything clever."

"Clever?" the Old Judge said with a smile. "I'm too old to do anything clever."

Anna followed at a discreet distance as the Old Judge stepped into his front garden and crossed to a large tree where the king waited silently. General Liddell glanced at Anna and gestured for her to stay back. His face registered a moment's recognition, but then he ignored her.

The king bowed slightly to the Old Judge. "Hello, you old fox," he said.

"Greetings, my son," the Old Judge replied as he nodded.

"My royal army doctors are up to their eyeballs in soldiers," the king said. "One regiment seems to be suffering from severe cramps from laughing too hard. The other can barely see from the soreness in their eyes. Do you know anything about it?"

The Old Judge spread his arms. "What could I know?" he asked.

"Just as I thought," the king said. "Where is Darien?"

"Hither and yon," the Old Judge answered.

"He's under suspicion of treason. You would be committing a crime by harboring a fugitive."

"Committing a crime against whom?"

"Against your king."

"*My* king? And who, pray tell, is *my* king? You know to whom I pledge allegiance, and it is no king that I see here."

Lawrence's face turned bright red, and he quickly pulled his sword from its sheath. He pointed it at the Old Judge's neck. "I'm not some fool that you can make laugh or cry, old one!" the king spat. "It would be within my right and my strength to strike you down here and now."

"Within your strength, perhaps," the Old Judge said coolly. "But not within your right. You waived that right when you turned your back on the Unseen One."

"The Unseen One turned His back on *me*," the king snarled.

The Old Judge frowned. "Is that so? Shall I recall your rebellion in front of this small audience? Do you want your general and this young girl to hear how you willfully disobeyed the One who made you king? I have held my tongue until now, Lawrence, but I will not hesitate to tell the world how you betrayed the ancient ways. And in betraying them, you have betrayed your own people. Where the blessings of the Unseen One could have been a harvest in your life, His curses will now fall upon you in ways you cannot comprehend!"

The king quivered for a moment as if he might thrust his sword through the Old Judge. The Old Judge simply blinked. An apple fell from the tree and hit the king on the top of his head.

The king looked up, perplexed. "This is no apple tree," he said. Another apple fell and hit him. Then another. And another. Soon it was raining apples on him. He ran away from the tree. The apple shower followed him. He began to laugh at the absurdity of the situation. Quickly, though, his laughter became uncontrollable. Then tears poured from his eyes. The king was laughing and crying at the same time. He gasped, desperate for breath.

General Liddell pointed his pistol at the Old Judge. "Stop it," he ordered, "or I'll kill you."

"Kill me and it will never stop until the king himself is

dead," the Old Judge responded with a steely gaze.

General Liddell returned the pistol to his belt and asked, "Then what do you want me to do?"

"Take the king away and he'll soon be back to his sour self," the Old Judge instructed. "And never—*never*—return to my cottage. The day that you do will be your last."

General Liddell, obviously shaken, helped the king, still helpless from his laughter and tears, get onto his horse. Once Lawrence had mounted, he brokenly said to the Old Judge, "Your conjurings won't stop me, old man. I will find Darien."

"Perhaps Darien will find *you*," the Old Judge said.

King Lawrence and General Liddell galloped away.

When the dust of the road had faded into the air, the Old Judge turned to Anna. "I have a mission for you," he said.

Balmovia, the king's country mansion, was a sprawling estate with acres and acres of royal forest, marshes, and groves inhabited by royal deer, rabbits, badgers, and other woodland animals. The forest rolled like a thick green carpet to the mansion itself, which stood on top of a hill. The house had more than 100 rooms, a grand banquet hall, a huge library, and endless corridors. It sat on a well-manicured lawn with gardens, adjoining tennis courts, a swimming pool, a maze of intricately carved shrubs, and an archery range. Because the woods were thickest on the side approaching the archery range, that's where Darien and Kyle ventured first.

"Considering the king's life is supposed to be in danger, they don't seem to have many guards around," Darien observed.

Kyle also noticed the absence of soldiers, police, or security guards watching the area. It seemed that Darien and he could have strolled in as if nothing had ever happened at the banquet the night before.

Through the trees, they could see that someone was practicing on the archery range. They heard the sound of the arrows sailing through the air and the dull thuds of the sharp points hitting a solid target.

"Maybe you should hide here while I go ahead," Kyle suggested. "If they see me, it won't matter. They're not looking for me. But everyone around the house will be watching for you."

Darien deferred to Kyle's idea. "I'll be here," he said.

Kyle crept to the edge of the forest, staying close to the ground. He hid behind a large tree and peered around it, which gave him a clear view of the field. His heart started to race. Prince George was alone, shooting at the target. Kyle looked up toward the house to see whether anyone there might spot him if he came out to signal George. The angle from the house would make the view difficult if not impossible.

Kyle waited until the prince exhausted his quiver of arrows, then stepped out into the open. At first George looked annoyed at the intruder. "What do you want?" he demanded.

"To speak to Your Highness on behalf of a friend," Kyle said.

George squinted at Kyle, and then his face brightened with recognition. "Kyle! Good heavens, boy, what are you doing here? Is—?" He stopped himself and looked around to be sure no one could see or hear him. "Is Darien all right?"

"Follow me and you'll see," Kyle replied.

George obeyed, following Kyle to where Darien had hidden.

Darien bowed to George and said, "My prince."

George grabbed Darien and embraced him heartily. "What are you doing here?" he asked. "Why have you taken this risk? I had hoped you'd be miles from here by now."

"I had to see you. To be sure."

"I'm so sorry about what's happened," George said. "I'm

afraid my father has lost his mind."

"So you don't believe the allegations in the *Sarum Herald*," Darien said, relieved.

George looked indignant. "Of course not!" he said. "I'm not privy to my father's scheming, but I knew he'd gone over the edge when he took a shot at you with that crossbow. I can't imagine what he was thinking."

"You're certain it wasn't an accident? He'd been drinking. . . ."

George frowned at his friend. "Didn't I warn you that something like this might happen? He's beside himself with jealousy. I believe something snapped when he heard the crowds calling your name beneath the balcony. All that nonsense in the newspaper was probably concocted by General Liddell."

Darien sat down on a log. He sighed heavily. "Then the king wants me dead."

"Dead or arrested," George said. "Though I doubt there's much difference between the two."

The two men were silent for a moment.

"Look, Darien, you have to get out of here—and out of the country," George continued. "You're not safe here at all. My father won't make a public spectacle of his desire to get rid of you, but he'll work quietly. He'll send his men after you. He already has, in fact. They went to the Old Judge's cottage to find you."

"Where can I go?" Darien asked sadly. "This is my homeland."

"I don't know," George replied with equal sorrow. He gave his mustache a quick brush with the side of his finger. "How about Prince Edwin? The people of Gotthard have always been friendly to you. Remember the fuss they made when you vacationed there last year? You were a celebrity. Prince Edwin himself couldn't do enough for you."

The idea seemed to appeal to Darien. "If he can give me refuge until your father's mind changes, maybe that will be enough."

"It's certainly worth a try," George said. "But I'd stay away from the trains or main roads. My father has spies everywhere."

A twig snapped loudly nearby. Darien, George, and Kyle all jumped and turned quickly to see if someone was sneaking up on them. It was a deer.

"You must go," George said, turning back to Darien. "It was foolish to come here."

"I couldn't have left the area without knowing for certain that we were still friends, no matter what happens with your father."

George clasped Darien's hand in his. "Our friendship is secure, my brother," he said with feeling. "May the Unseen One be our witness."

"So be it," Darien said, smiling.

"Now go," the prince urged.

Back at the Old Judge's cottage, everyone sat down for dinner. While they ate, Anna told Darien and Kyle about what had happened to the king's soldiers and then to the king himself. Kyle was astounded.

Darien cast a troubled glance at the Old Judge. "Is it appropriate to torment the king of our country that way?" he asked.

The Old Judge snorted impatiently. "You deal with the

king in your way and I'll deal with him in mine," he replied. "Remember, son, that I have known him much longer than you have."

Darien didn't reply to that but said, "It's time to leave. I want to go first to see that my family is all right. After that, I'll travel to Gotthard. Prince George believes that Edwin and his people will receive me."

"So they might," the Old Judge said. "There is a remnant of believers in the Unseen One there."

"You agree?" Darien asked, surprised.

"Why wouldn't I?" the Old Judge asked.

"I thought you would probably have another plan worked out—something better from the Unseen One."

"Something easy, perhaps?"

"Yes."

"A quick snap of the fingers and everything will be taken care of?"

Darien nodded. "It would be easy enough for the Unseen One."

"Easy, yes," the Old Judge said with a smile. "But the Unseen One rarely makes things easy for us."

"Why not?" Kyle asked.

"Because the Unseen One knows our hearts. When we are given things easily, we dismiss them easily. When the Unseen One makes us work and sweat and struggle a little for what we have, we respect and treasure it." He turned to Darien. "You will respect your crown when you have struggled to win it." His face then went dark. "But even your respect will not be enough to keep it on your head."

Darien groaned. "I'm not even king yet and you're predicting trouble?"

"I predict nothing," the Old Judge said. "Know this,

however: For all your attributes, Darien, there are weaknesses. Beware your weaknesses. There are those who wait to see them and exploit them."

Darien waved the warning away. "Enough of this talk," he said. "I have a long journey ahead of me."

The Old Judge clasped his hands under his chin. "All of you do," he said.

"All of us?" Darien asked.

Anna suddenly realized what the Old Judge was saying. "Me, too?" she said.

"Darien, I would like you to make your journey past the town of Dorr," the Old Judge instructed. "There's a convent there. Go to Sister Leona. She can help you. It's important, though, that you don't explain to her *why* you're traveling."

"Then why would I want to go there?" asked Darien.

"Because I want Anna to stay with her."

"What?" Anna cried out. "Why?"

The Old Judge reached over, laid a hand on her arm, and explained, "Because your gift is still new and hasn't been properly developed."

"Gift?" Anna's face went alternately red, then white, then red again.

"Do you really think I don't know about the dreams and visions you've been having?"

Anna's mouth fell open. "You know about that?"

"My dear child, why do you think you are here?" The Old Judge asked the question as if the answer should have been obvious to everyone. He didn't elaborate further but said, "Now you must go to Sister Leona, for she will help you with your gift."

Anna looked puzzled. "How?" she asked.

"You'll find out when the time is right."

Darien stood up, along with Kyle. "We must leave if we hope to make it to Dorr before daybreak," Darien said.

Anna hesitated. She knew she had to leave the Old Judge. And only now did she realize how deeply she cared for him. "But sir . . ." she began. She searched for words that wouldn't come. "I don't want to say good-bye."

"Nor do I," he said warmly. "You have been a breath of fresh air to me, a beautiful light. But it's necessary that you go."

"Will we come back?" she asked. "Will I see you again?"

"We are in the hands of the Unseen One. I make no promises, but I hope that one day we will." His eyes suddenly filled with tears. "I do not envy you your journey, child. It will not be without its share of suffering. But often it is in suffering that we see the ancient ways of the Unseen One most clearly."

Anna struggled to keep back her tears as they walked to the front door. She hugged the Old Judge quickly. "Thank you," she said.

"You're welcome," he replied warmly.

Darien shook the Old Judge's hand with silent gratitude. Kyle did the same.

The shadows of dusk surrounded them as they crossed from the house to the edge of the forest. Darien and Kyle looked back to wave at the Old Judge, who stood in the doorway, framed with golden light. Anna kept her eyes forward.

The three travelers had an uneventful journey and arrived at the village of Dorr shortly before morning. It had been a long walk, and Kyle and Anna were exhausted. The only thing either of them wanted was a bed.

The convent the Old Judge had mentioned sat on the village outskirts. It was a modest stone compound with high walls and a huge door on the front. Darien banged the simple iron knocker several times. Five minutes passed before a young, sleepy-eyed girl wearing a hood opened the door. When Darien introduced himself, the girl stumbled and stammered that they should wait right there while she went to get Sister Leona. She disappeared into a dark corridor.

Sister Leona, the head of the convent, came to the door in her dressing gown. Her white hair was tousled and stuck out at odd angles under her hood. Her eyes were puffy from sleep. "Come in, come in!" she said and led them in. They took a path through a beautiful courtyard with flowers and a fountain and eventually arrived at a small building on the other side of the enclosure. It housed a primitive kitchen and long, wooden table. Sister Leona and another girl quickly warmed up a meat stew, even though Darien assured her it wasn't necessary.

After the food had been served and a blessing said, Sister Leona turned to Anna. Her eyes were piercing in their intensity. "So the Old Judge wants me to teach you?" she said. "You must be very special for him to send you to me."

Anna blushed and said, "I don't know what he thinks I'll learn."

"You'll learn what you're willing to learn," Sister Leona answered. Anna then noticed that, like the Old Judge, Sister Leona's eyes were two different colors—one blue, the other green. "Is there something wrong?" she asked.

Anna averted her gaze. "No, ma'am."

"General Darien, why are you traveling so late at night— and without your attendants and soldiers?" asked Sister Leona. "Are you on your way to a battle?"

"No, Sister," Darien replied and ate some bread. Kyle and Anna exchanged uneasy glances.

"Had we known you were going to visit our humble convent, we would have made proper arrangements for you," Sister Leona said. "Normally an official at the king's palace informs us when—"

Darien interrupted her: "The king's officials aren't involved in this enterprise. This is a secret mission."

"Then the allegations that you are part of a plot against the king are false?"

"I can assure you that they are false. I am not part of a plot against the king." Darien toyed with his bread. "As it happens, we were passing this way, so the Old Judge asked us to bring Anna to you. That's all. It would be helpful if you didn't ask any more questions."

"I see," Sister Leona said politely. "Is there anything I can give you for your mission? More food?"

"Beds for a couple of hours' sleep would be most appreciated."

"Anything else?"

"A pistol and a sword," Darien said as a joke. "I'm traveling without my weapons."

Sister Leona didn't laugh. She merely tapped her chin with her index finger. "I may be able to help you with one of those items," she said seriously.

A few minutes later, they were in Sister Leona's private study. On the wall above the fireplace hung a large golden sword. Darien reached up, unclasped it, and carefully brought it down. "Amazing!" he said softly. "I had no idea it was here."

"Is there something special about it?" Kyle asked.

"It's the sword that belonged to Commander Soren of the Palatians," Sister Leona explained.

Kyle looked at the sword with awe and said, "You mean the one the commander used to try to kill General Darien?"

"The very one."

Darien held the sword up. The light from the gas lamps caught the edges of the sword, sending thin beams of yellow in all directions. "How did you come by it?" he asked.

"It was a gift to our order from the king," Sister Leona said. She searched a nearby closet and pulled out the sword's belt and sheath. "But it is yours by right, General. If you need it for your secret mission, then you must take it."

"I'll borrow it," Darien said.

They slept only a couple of hours before Darien was ready to move on to his family's farm. He woke Kyle up first, then together they went to Anna's room to say good-bye. She sat up in her bed and rubbed her eyes sleepily. When she realized they were leaving her, she was immediately distressed. "I'm afraid," she whispered to her brother.

"So am I," he admitted. "But it's probably a good idea for you to stay here."

"What if something happens to you?"

"I'm the protector," he said as bravely as he could. "Nothing can happen to me."

Neither of them believed it, but they didn't say so.

"How will I know where you are?" she asked. "How will I find you?"

"*We'll* find you," Darien assured her. "Or we'll send for you."

Kyle smiled. "Yeah, we'll send somebody with a secret code. He'll say: *Uncle Bill wants to see you.*"

"That's silly," Anna said.

Kyle nodded. "Yep," he agreed.

Darien put a hand on Kyle's shoulder. "The sun is up," he said. "We have to go." Then he left the room. Kyle lingered, looked at his sister with a worried expression, then spun on his heel and left.

Anna buried her face in her pillow and prayed to the Unseen One, "Please don't let anything happen to them."

Darien and Kyle walked around the village of Dorr, staying close to the outlying fields so they wouldn't be spotted. The only living creatures they ran into were a flock of sheep and their shepherd. Darien said hello to the shepherd as if they were on a morning stroll rather than a couple of fugitives on the run. The shepherd smiled back and said "Good morning" pleasantly.

Kyle felt that sick feeling in the pit of his stomach again

and immediately prepared himself for something bad to happen. Maybe the shepherd was going to attack Darien with his crook. The shepherd just looked curiously at him, however, then walked on. *That's strange,* Kyle thought. *Is my "protector antenna" going wrong?*

Anna, asleep in her bed, saw the encounter with the shepherd in a dream. But she also saw what Darien and Kyle didn't: The shepherd waited until they were out of sight and then ran to the village. In her dream, she felt peaceful and unalarmed. When she awoke, however, her heart beat furiously in her chest. Panicked, she looked around her room. The thick curtains on the single window were drawn. The small wooden washstand, the bedside table, and the rectangular brown carpet on the floor all seemed to be cast in a single shadow. Suddenly the door was thrown open and a man rushed in, his sword drawn. Before Anna could scream, he ran her through in a single thrust.

And then she was truly awake. It had been another dream. Her room was filled with the half light of a sunny day that pushed through the drawn curtains. The door was closed.

She tried to figure out what the two dreams meant but didn't know how. Chilled and feverish, her eyes burning in their sockets, she tried to stand up. Her legs gave way, and she collapsed onto the floor.

That's where Sister Leona found her later in the morning.

"Father!" Darien cried as he and his father embraced.

The stooped and bearded old man held his son. "Darien!" he exclaimed.

His mother joined the embrace as the three clung to one another.

It was late afternoon, and the four of them met in a small cabin on the outer limits of Darien's family property. Just in case King Lawrence had people watching, Kyle had run ahead to the back door of the house to secretly tell Darien's parents where their son was. "Tell him to meet us at the old house after dark," his father had instructed.

"Is it safe?" Kyle had asked.

"No one but our family has any idea it's there," Darien's father had replied. "I am Torbin, by the way. This is my wife, Evelyn. You must be my son's guardian angel."

Kyle had nodded as a reply and said, "We'll see you there after dark."

He had run back to deliver the message to Darien. They had then made their way to the old house, so called because it was where Darien's ancestors had lived when they first settled the land. It was a one-room cabin that reminded Kyle of an oversized playhouse. Inside were a few items of furniture—a cot, sofa, and kitchen table—and not much else. The cot had captured Kyle's eye first. He was tired and felt as if he'd been in a relay race most of the day. All he wanted to do was stretch out and rest while Darien conversed with his parents around the small kitchen table. So he did.

"The king's men were here yesterday," Darien's father said, his tanned face wrinkled and folded like a plowed field. "They're probably watching now, too. But we were too smart for them. I had two servants dress like us and ride to town while we slipped out the back door."

"Is everyone all right?" Darien asked. "Did the king's men do anything to you?"

"Oh, they were abusive and pushed us around a little,

but nothing serious," Torbin said.

"They broke my mother's china," Evelyn complained. "The bullies!"

"They could've broken more than that," Torbin said.

"How about the rest of the family?" Darien asked.

His father rubbed his beard absentmindedly. "They are well. They're wondering what brought this on. Why would the king suddenly turn on you?"

"He thinks I want his job," Darien said wryly.

"Ah," Darien's mother said. "Then he knows about our visit from the Old Judge."

Darien shrugged. "Maybe he does."

"Or maybe he's worried because of your success as a general," Torbin suggested.

"This is terrible! Just terrible!" said Evelyn. "You never should have left the farm. If you'd stayed here with your family, none of this would've happened!"

Darien reached over and stroked his mother's face. "My place was not on this farm," he told her. "I was called to other things."

"Yes," Evelyn said with a frown. "And one day I will have words with the Unseen One about that!"

Darien ignored her comment and said, "Meanwhile, we have to be sure you're safe. I think the prince of Gotthard will give you sanctuary until we can sort out this mess."

"Gotthard! You want us to leave our farm?" Torbin asked.

"I don't see that we have a choice. The king may decide to punish you as a means to get to me. So you must pack your things while I try to make contact with the prince on your behalf."

"On our behalf? You're not coming with us?" Evelyn asked, her voice laced with worry.

Darien shook his head. "The prince can give you refuge without much trouble. To help me directly would threaten his relationship with King Lawrence. What with their various treaties and agreements, he dare not take the chance. I will find other places to hide."

"Other places to hide . . ." Torbin groaned and hit the table angrily. Kyle opened an eye to look at them. "The greatest general in our land, and you have to hide. May the Unseen One see our plight and deliver us from this madness!"

Darien agreed, "And so He may. But until He does, we have to take every precaution."

Kyle reluctantly gave up the cot to follow Darien and his parents outside. While Kyle waited on the porch, Darien hugged and kissed his mother and father good night. Then they began the long walk home across the field. It was a beautiful summer's night. The chirping crickets and flashing fireflies went about their business as if the world hadn't been turned upside down for this family. Darien and Kyle watched Torbin and Evelyn until they disappeared over the dark horizon.

"Now, how am I going to get in touch with Prince Edwin?" Darien muttered as he turned to go back inside the cabin. Suddenly, without warning, a loud shout seemed to come from all around them. Darien quickly reached for his sword, forgetting that he'd left it inside. It was too late anyway. They were surrounded.

"A man of your experience should be more on his guard," a voice said. From the darkness of the woods, Colonel Oliver approached carrying a torch. Like phantoms bearing candles, almost 100 of Darien's most faithful soldiers came forward.

"What are you doing here, Colonel?" Darien asked after briskly shaking his hand. He was amazed. "How in the world did you find this place?"

"The Old Judge sent the girl to me a few nights ago," Colonel Oliver said.

"Anna?" Darien asked.

"Yes. She told us where and when to meet you. I got the word around to those I knew would want to come."

"But *what* are you doing here?" asked Darien.

"We're with you, sir," Colonel Oliver said resolutely. "Wherever you go, we go. None of us desire to serve under any other commander, even if he *is* supposed to be a scoundrel and a traitor."

Darien looked around at the faces of the men, knowing well what they were sacrificing for him. "I cannot ask you to do this," he said in a choked voice.

Colonel Oliver nodded. "Nor do we expect you to ask," he said matter-of-factly. "Which is why we've come of our own free will. Now, are we going to stand here all night or are you going to tell us what you need us to do?"

They spent most of the night discussing their options. Having so many men to help made all the difference in Darien's attitude. He became a general again.

Kyle sat on the edge of the cot, knowing he wouldn't be able to sleep now. Instead he wondered about Anna—the bold errand girl for the Old Judge. Somehow she seemed so different from the whiny little sister he had wanted to desert before this adventure began. He hoped she was being well treated at the convent.

Sister Leona took care of Anna personally. She fed her soup and spoke gently to her while dabbing her forehead with a

cool, damp cloth. Anna felt as if she was constantly drift-
ing between her dreams and reality—to the point where she
wasn't sure which was which.

"The Ancient Fathers and Mothers had dreams," Sister
Leona said. Though they had only begun to talk, Anna had
the feeling that they had been chatting for hours and this was
a conversation in the middle of it all. "The Unseen One used
dreams to speak to the chosen ones. Only a handful are left
who have the dreams or know how to interpret them. These
are the days of abandonment, when the leaders and their people turn away from the ancient ways and the Unseen One."

"I don't like my dreams," Anna said through a voice
like sandpaper.

"No. Few of us do." Sister Leona wrung the cloth out,
then reapplied it to Anna's face. "To be a voice for the Unseen
One can be a great burden. Sometimes it involves suffering—even sharing the suffering of others. But our faith in
the Unseen One carries us through. Do you have that kind
of faith, Anna?"

"I want to."

"Then feed that faith with prayer and study, silence and
solitude. Will you do that?"

Anna closed her eyes. "I'll do my best."

When she opened her eyes again, the room was empty.

She slept until evening. Sister Leona knocked gently on
the door, then walked in. She wore a cloak, as if she were
about to leave.

"How are you feeling, Anna?" she asked.

Anna took a deep breath. The burning in her eyes had
stopped. She felt weak but much better and said so.

"Good," said Sister Leona, taking Anna's hand and sitting
beside her on the bed.

"Have we been talking?" Anna asked.

"A little," Sister Leona said.

"Then it was a dream. I dreamed we talked a lot."

Sister Leona smiled and patted her hand. "I hope it was a pleasant dream," she said. Then she stood up and explained, "I have to leave for a while. I've been summoned."

"Summoned?"

"The king has come to Dorr and asked to see me."

"King Lawrence?"

"There is no other king that I know of."

Anna sat up quickly. Her head spun. "Sister . . . I had a dream about soldiers and swords and . . ." She couldn't bring herself to say the word *death*. "And danger," she said.

"We'll talk about it when I return," Sister Leona said. "In a little while."

"Will you also teach me?" Anna asked. "The Old Judge said you would teach me how to use my gift—and you'd give me something."

"You have all you need," said the sister with a knowing smile. She handed a small mirror to Anna and left.

Anna wasn't sure what she was supposed to do with the mirror. Was she supposed to say "Mirror, mirror on the wall"? She looked at her reflection. Her face was pale and gaunt. Her eyes sat atop dark circles. *Her eyes!* Her entire life she'd had brown eyes. Now they were two separate colors; one was blue and the other green. She put a hand to her mouth as if to stop her sudden intake of breath. She stared at them, unsure what to think.

After a moment, Anna lay back in her bed. The wheels of her mind spun wildly, and her heart raced. *What does this mean?* she wondered. She heard voices whispering in the hallway, and then a young girl walked in. She was pretty, with long, braided hair and freckles on her nose. She said her name was Dawn and that Sister Leona wanted her to sit with Anna for a while.

"I don't need anyone to sit with me," Anna said. "I'm all right."

Dawn reached over and touched Anna's forehead tenderly. "Are you sure?" she asked.

"Yes, I am," she replied, and then she fell asleep again.

Her dreams were fitful. In them she saw Sister Leona walk down a dingy hallway and into a room with candles and lamps set up in odd places, as if the room normally wouldn't have so much light. The walls were covered with cheap paintings and documents that looked like legal papers and diplomas. A rolltop desk, also covered with papers, sat in the corner. In the center of the room, King Lawrence leaned back in a large thronelike chair that didn't belong in the office at all. On one side of him stood a short, bald-headed man who kept wringing his hands. On the other side, General Liddell stood as straight as any ruler. Sister Leona knelt out of respect for the king, then waited.

"Get up, get up," the king commanded wearily.

Anna was surprised because this was the first time she'd had a dream about the king where she could hear him clearly.

"What can I do for you, sire?" Sister Leona asked when she stood up.

The king rested his elbow on the arm of the chair and his hand against the side of his face. "Tell me about General Darien," he said.

Sister Leona looked puzzled. "General Darien?"

"Don't play innocent with me," he said. "General Darien came to see you last night. Or should I say earlier this morning? What did he want? Why was he here?"

Sister Leona glanced around nervously. "Your Highness should know better than I would."

"Indeed? Tell me what I should know."

"General Darien is on a secret mission. That's as much as he said. I assumed it was a mission for you."

"Were you not aware that he is suspected of being a traitor?" the king asked.

"The newspapers hinted at the idea, but I haven't seen any official papers or warrants for his arrest. I'd be a fool to believe everything I read in the newspaper. Besides, General Darien denied it."

"He would deny it, wouldn't he?" the king scoffed.

"He would if he were a liar," Sister Leona said. "But I have no reason to think he'd lie."

The king jerked forward in his chair. His eyes were aflame, his face twisted into a scowl. "Yet you would believe your king to be a liar!"

"Why would you say such a thing to me?" said Sister Leona indignantly. "I'm a loyal subject."

"Are you?" the king bellowed. "Then explain to me what you, my loyal subject, did for General Darien!"

"Did for him? I don't know what you mean."

The king waved his hand. "Oram!"

A tall, hairy man dressed in a vest of sheepskin stepped from a corner behind Sister Leona. "Yes, Your Highness?" he said.

"She doesn't understand me. Please enlighten her."

"Eh?"

"Say what you know!" the king commanded impatiently.

"Oh," he said, shuffling his feet like a small child. "Well, like I told you, sire, I was walking this morning with my flock, and I saw General Darien and a boy walking from the sister's convent. We said hello in a friendly manner. I knew it was Darien but acted like I didn't because I read in the paper how he might be plotting against you. And then I saw that he was wearing a long gold sword. So I thought, *Hold on, that's the sword that was in the sister's study,* 'cause I seen it there myself when I had business in the place once or twice. I was then wondering if maybe the general didn't rob the sister of the sword. So I ran to Phipps here, our magistrate—"

With this acknowledgment, the bald-headed man nodded.

"—and he told me he'd contact you if I went to the convent to see if it'd been robbed. Well, I happen to know one of the girls there—she's one of the few girls who'll give me the time of day, the rest being holy snobs and all—and I asked her right away what was up with General Darien. Did he come in the night to rob them? And she said that the sword wasn't stolen but *given* to General Darien by Sister Leona, along with some food."

The king gestured to Sister Leona as if to say, "Well?"

Sister Leona said firmly, "Are you accusing me of something?"

"Apart from giving food and a weapon to my sworn enemy, then no, I don't suppose I am!" the king shouted ironically. His face had turned bright red.

Sister Leona didn't flinch, and her voice remained calm. "General Darien has been an honorable and dutiful servant to you. I had no reason to think he was otherwise. What I did for him, I did because I believed him to be on a mission for you. If there were more to know or reasons to distrust him, they are beyond me."

"*Beyond* you? I thought you prophets for the Unseen One knew everything!"

"We don't."

"That is truly unfortunate," the king sneered. "Now get out of my sight."

Sister Leona said in a stern voice, "Your Highness—"

"Go!" he screamed at her.

She bowed slightly and walked out.

The king leaped out of his chair and prowled around the room. "These people—these believers in the Unseen One—will all side with Darien against me. I know it!" he said. "We have to send a message to them. They have to understand that I will not tolerate their treason!"

"What kind of message, sire?" General Liddell asked.

"I want those sisters killed. Every last one of them."

General Liddell stared at the king in disbelief. "Killed! No, sire, that would be extreme," he cautioned.

"Did I hear you say no to me?" the king asked menacingly. "Is that what I heard?"

General Liddell changed his tone. "Sire, as your loyal general, I can only say that such a move would be disastrous. If anyone saw members of the Royal Guard committing such an act, the entire nation would turn against them—and you. It could spark an uprising that none of us could contain."

The king clasped his hands behind his back and growled, "Then get somebody else to do it! I want it done, and I want it done by tonight!" The king left no time for answers or questions as he stomped out of the room. Phipps the magistrate followed anxiously.

General Liddell folded his arms, his face a frozen mask. He then looked at the shepherd. "Oram?" he said.

"Yes, sir?"

"The convent owns a lot of the land around here, doesn't it?"

"Too much, if you ask me."

"You'd like that land for your sheep, wouldn't you?" Liddell's voice was oily with opportunity. "Imagine all the grazing they could do."

"Yes, sir. I've imagined it. Even talked to the lady—that one in charge—but she wouldn't agree."

"You've heard what the king wants done. Can you do it quickly, in exchange for the land?"

Oram's expression didn't change. "Me and the boys can do it right away. Never cared for those women and all that nonsense about the Unseen Thingy watching over us anyway. Dangerous superstition, I figure."

"Dangerous—yes," the general said.

Anna woke up. Dawn sat next to the bed, reading a book. Her lips moved ever so slightly. She was praying.

"Dawn," Anna said with a parched throat.

Dawn put a finger to her lips. "Wait. I'll get you something to drink," she offered.

"No," Anna said. Her voice rose as the panic within her grew. "Something awful is going to happen."

The door opened slightly, and Sister Leona peered in. "Ah, you're awake," she said.

"Sister Leona! I just had a dream," Anna said quickly. "You were with the king."

Sister Leona began to take off her cloak. "You knew I was going to see him," she said.

"He accused you of helping General Darien," Anna said.

A shadow crossed Sister Leona's face. Her voice took on a tone of urgency. "What else did you see in the dream?"

"They're coming."

"Who is?"

"The shepherd. He's coming to—"

In another part of the building, there was a loud crash.

Someone screamed.

"Wait here," Sister Leona said. "Both of you. And lock this door behind me." She rushed out of the room, closing the door behind her.

Dawn moved nervously to the door and locked it. More screams echoed through the halls, increasing in number and intensity. "Mercy!" Dawn whispered.

Anna crawled out of the bed. Her clothes were neatly folded on the bottom shelf of the bedside table. She grabbed them and dressed as quickly as she could.

Men's voices intermingled with the screams. They came closer down the hall. Sister Leona shouted at someone, but her voice was suddenly silenced. Dawn began to cry as she backed away from the door. Anna threw the curtains aside. The window frame was small, but it looked as if she and Dawn could squeeze through.

"We have to get out of here," Anna said.

"What's happening?" Dawn cried. "What are they doing?"

"They're going to kill us!" shouted Anna. The latch on the window stubbornly refused to move. It probably hadn't been opened in years. The shouts and screams came closer and closer.

"Have mercy!" Dawn said again, her hand to her mouth. Someone was at the door. The handle moved up and down quickly. A man shouted.

Anna tugged at the window latch with all her might. It gave a little and then completely. She threw open the window just as someone began to beat against the door. The old wooden frame splintered, and the door handle broke loose.

"Hurry, Dawn!" Anna screamed.

Trancelike, Dawn drifted toward the door. Her hand reached out. "No," she said softly.

The frame gave way to the blows of whoever was on the other side. A large man burst in, surveyed the room in a glance, and caught Dawn by the hair. He drew his sword back.

Instinctively, Anna grabbed the lamp on the bedside table and threw it at him. It crashed against his side, the fuel catching his sheepskin vest on fire. He yelled angrily and ran his sword into Dawn. She fell at his feet. The man staggered toward Anna, then swung out and caught her on the side of the head with his fist. She fell back against the wall. The man threw himself onto the bed, squirming and writhing to put out the flames. He had little success as the flames spread to other areas of his clothing, then onto the bed itself.

Anna scrambled for the window.

The man's agonizing cries followed her as she fell from the window to a makeshift roof one story below. It gave way under her weight and she crashed through, landing on her side on a hay-covered dirt floor. A sharp pain shot through her hip and down her legs. Struggling to her feet, she half ran and half limped away from the convent and into the night.

CHAPTER

11

Word came to Darien, then Kyle, about the massacre at the Dorr convent through one of Darien's soldiers. The blame was placed on unknown marauders and vandals who killed the women, then set fire to the building. There were no witnesses to claim otherwise. General Liddell, who visited the scene of the destruction, promised a full investigation into the tragedy. "Justice will be served," he proclaimed on the steps of the burned-out shell.

"Anna! What about Anna?" Kyle asked urgently.

"There were no survivors," Darien replied, his hand held firmly on Kyle's shoulder.

Kyle's voice trembled. "No. I don't believe it!" he insisted. "We didn't come here for Anna to die! I have to see for myself!"

Darien signaled Colonel Oliver. "It's only a couple of hours on horseback. Will you take him?" he asked.

Colonel Oliver nodded and went to saddle the horses. Kyle closed his eyes to fight back his tears. *What kind of world is this?* he asked himself. *The Unseen One wouldn't allow Anna to die!*

Dorr was crowded with soldiers from the royal army. Though the king and General Liddell had left, government officials and detectives remained to ask questions and make a good showing of sympathy to those who'd died. Grieving relatives arrived to identify their dead daughters who had joined the convent in high hopes of serving the Unseen One with their lives. In a way, Kyle thought, they had.

The stone walls of the convent stood tall, as if nothing had happened. But the wooden beams that held up the roof, the frames around the windows, and the large oak doors were all gone or turned into fallen black sticks of no distinction. Kyle's heart sank as he looked at the charred ruins. The local police wouldn't let them any closer than the gate. Phipps, the local magistrate, was keeping a tight seal on the area.

Colonel Oliver used his influence with a friend in the army to get a list of those who'd been found in the convent. He scanned it, then handed it over to Kyle. Breathlessly, Kyle ran his finger along the names of those who'd been claimed and the descriptions of those who hadn't. None of them fit Anna.

"She's not here," Kyle said, afraid to hope.

"Are you sure?" Colonel Oliver asked.

Kyle tapped the list. "It says that all these girls were teenagers or older. Anna isn't here!"

"I got the impression that she's a very resourceful girl," Colonel Oliver said. "Maybe she escaped."

Kyle scanned the crowds nearby, the town, and the rolling green fields around them. Dark clouds were moving in. "Then where did she go?" he asked.

It began to rain.

The rain tapped like impatient fingers on the top of the old tin roof. Anna opened her eyes and immediately recoiled from the squalor of the place. A makeshift sink was filled with dishes and rotten food; a nearby rat sniffed at it with disdain. The walls and floor were made of loose-fitting boards that easily let weather, dust, and mud through. She thought she heard the buzzing of flies nearby. Looking down, she realized she was on a bed of straw.

She groaned as she reached for her aching head. It was bruised and tender to touch. Swinging her legs over the side of the bed, she winced. Her hip and legs also hurt. The pain worked through the fuzziness of her head, and she remembered what had happened at the convent. She stifled a cry, resolved to be strong, and instantly prayed to the Unseen One for the families of those who had died, for she knew without a doubt that everyone had—particularly Sister Leona and Dawn.

Only afterward did she realize how strange, yet natural, it was for her to pray at all.

"Hello there, little one," a croaking old voice said.

Anna looked up. A shriveled old woman in a patched-up peasant dress and shawl walked in. She was hunched over as she carried a bucket and still hunched after she put it down next to the lopsided, wooden table. Her dirty gray hair dripped with rain but looked as if it might drip even in the sunshine.

"I wouldn't get up too fast if I was ye," the old woman said.

"Who are you?" Anna asked. "Where am I?"

"Ye're in the house of Anastasia—*my* house," the old woman said happily. "I lives near Wollet-in-Stone. Stumbling around in the dark, ye were. Thought ye were a beggar, I·did. Nearly turned ye away, excepting I had a torch and saw yer eyes. Then I knew better. Better indeed. Ye walked miles."

"What do *you* care about my eyes?"

The old woman named Anastasia poked a bony finger toward Anna's face. "Two colors, ye have. One of the marks of the Unseen One. 'She's special,' I said to myself and put ye to bed. Bad luck otherwise. I found foreign coins in yer pockets. They will serve as payment for my help." She held out a quarter, a dime, and two nickels that Anna had been carrying.

Anna rubbed her eyes to be sure she wasn't in another dream.

"Ye said much in yer sleep," Anastasia went on. "Came from Sister Leona's holy house, I reckoned. Sister Leona never liked me, but I'm sad that she was made dead. A tragedy, it was. I heared that the king himself wept over the news."

Wept for joy, Anna thought and bit her tongue to keep from saying it. "Why didn't Sister Leona like you?" Anna asked instead. Her tongue felt numb, her speech slurred.

"Because I'm not like her, I'm not. I make a business that she don't approve of."

"What kind of business?"

The old woman laughed in a horselike manner. "Questions. So many questions ye have. The spirits of the departed is my trade. I speak to them and they visit me, they do."

Anna then noticed an old, faded carnival poster hanging on the wall. "Anastasia the Mysterious," it said in large, curly letters. Beneath it was a crudely rendered painting of a much younger Anastasia with her hair flowing and shimmering around a round face with magnetic eyes. Her hands were raised up as if she were conjuring something, her nails a bright blue. Anna shivered involuntarily. The rat at the sink eyed her for a moment as if it understood her feelings.

"It's the rain, isn't it? Ye're cold," Anastasia said. She walked to a rusted potbellied stove in the corner and stoked the tiny embers. They spat defiantly at her. "Warm ye up, this will."

Anna tested her legs to stand, and, though it hurt, she was pleased that she could. "Thank you for your kindness, but I have to find my brother," she said politely.

"Go? In this rain? Ye mustn't," Anastasia protested.

"But he'll be worried about me," Anna said, imagining how Kyle would react to the news about the convent. "He doesn't know where I am."

Anastasia sat down at the lopsided table and shuffled some cards. "Do ye know where he is?" she asked. "We can contact him without yer walks in the rain."

Frowning, Anna asked, "How?" *Card tricks? A séance? Maybe a crystal ball?* she wondered.

"Call."

"Call?" Anna asked, puzzled.

The old woman pointed to a box on the wall. It had thin, exposed wires running from the top and out through a hole in the wall. "Yes. It's called a telephone, it is. Have ye not heard of it?"

Placing Anna's call took some doing. First, an operator had to be called. That operator transferred Anna to another who handled inquiries about phone numbers. When Anna didn't know Darien's parents' names or in what town they lived, that operator then connected her to the Ministry of Information in Sarum. The clerk there was less than helpful when he realized Anna wanted information about General Darien's family. The palace had put a seal on any information related to General Darien. Anna tried to reason with the clerk. "It can't be *that* big of a secret," she said. Finally the clerk allowed that the general's family lived several miles from a town called Leapford. That was as much as he would say before he hung up on her.

"I could have told ye that," Anastasia said with a smirk on her face.

"Why didn't you?" Anna said.

"Ye didn't ask."

Anna went back to the operator who handled inquiries about phone numbers and asked about Darien's family's phone number in Leapford. The operator said she would have to connect her to the Leapford operator. Once that was done, the Leapford operator, who had been friends with Torbin and Evelyn for years, warily transferred Anna to what she called the "public line" for the house. A servant answered and promised to deliver Anna's message to either Torbin or Evelyn, though he claimed not to know anything about Darien or his whereabouts.

Anna hung up, exhausted from all the effort. *It would've been easier if I'd walked,* she thought.

Three things happened as a result of Anna's trip through the telephone maze. First, the servant told Torbin about the call from Anna. Torbin ventured out to the old house, where Darien and his men were making final preparations to leave for Gotthard. Darien dispatched Kyle and Colonel Oliver to go get Anna from the old woman's shack near Wollet-in-Stone.

Second, Kyle got a crash course in horseback riding, having his own mount for the first time.

And third, the Leapford operator told her boss about the call. The boss, who was under strict orders to report any activity connected to Darien's family, phoned the palace to tell them about the girl's call. This news, combined with another report from the Ministry of Information, told General Liddell that Darien must be somewhere near his parents. Liddell passed the news on to King Lawrence.

———✥———

Kyle hugged his sister without restraint or embarrassment there in front of the Wollet-in-Stone post office. It was the only building in the village. The rain had diminished to a light sprinkle.

"Ouch," Anna groaned, her entire body now one big pain.

"I knew you weren't dead," he said in her ear. "The Unseen One wouldn't let you die."

Anna smiled at her brother's affection and his conviction about the Unseen One. Somehow the two of them had gone from doubting His existence to faith that He was with them on this adventure.

"What happened to your eyes?" he asked.

"I'll tell you some other time."

Colonel Oliver, atop his horse, beckoned the two of them to hurry up. "General Darien is waiting for us," he reminded them.

Kyle rubbed his aching legs. "Okay. You ride with me," he told Anna.

"Not a chance," Anna said and climbed onto Colonel Oliver's horse.

Back at the old house, the three of them arrived to the chaos of Darien's family and army finalizing the preparations for their journey to Gotthard. Darien embraced Anna when he saw her, then took her and Kyle aside. He wanted to know what had happened at the convent.

"King Lawrence sent the men in to kill us," Anna said as the memory of her dreams and the attack returned to her. Her bottom lip quivered as she told him everything.

"I blame myself," Darien said angrily. "Those poor women and girls lost their lives because I visited them."

"But you only visited them because the Old Judge told you to," Kyle offered.

"The Old Judge told me to take Anna there—not stay for food or take Soren's sword. If I'd done exactly as he said, it wouldn't have happened."

Kyle and Anna watched Darien as he brooded. The business at hand demanded that he not brood for long.

"If I am ever made king," he finally said, "I will set these things to right. There will be justice in this land."

chapter

12

The rain moved on to other parts, but the journey to the Gotthard border still took most of the day. To Kyle's and Anna's relief, nothing bad happened. Kyle never felt that sick feeling in his stomach. Anna didn't have any troublesome dreams. The only real difficulty was Kyle's inexperience riding his own horse—a cantankerous old beast named Bethesda—and the added bruises it gave him.

Once at the border, Darien sadly said good-bye to his parents and handed them over to Prince Edwin's officials for safekeeping. Darien was assured, by letter from the prince, that they would be made comfortable and kept secure under royal protection in a secret location.

"I am proud of you, my son," Darien's father said. "Be strong."

"Be *safe*," Darien's mother added. She wept loudly as they rode away.

Darien and his officers decided to head south from Gotthard toward the section of Marus that adjoined Palatia, to a walled-in town called Kellen. It was large enough to accommodate the 100-strong regiment that traveled with Darien, but remote enough to hide them for a while. It also stood at the entrance to an area called the Valley of the

Rocks, a rough wilderness where they could escape if King Lawrence found them and decided to attack.

"Do you think he would be so obvious?" Colonel Oliver asked as they strategized. "You haven't been declared a criminal as such. Why would he take such direct action?"

"He sanctioned the massacre at the convent. He's capable of anything," replied Darien.

As they drew closer to the town that evening, the woods opened up to a long stretch of flat fields. Darien noticed that the road seemed unusually deserted. "This is the only paved road to this part of the country," he said. "One would think that it'd be busier."

Farther on, they saw that some of the telephone and telegraph poles had been knocked down, the lines cut.

"This looks awfully suspicious," Colonel Oliver noted. "I'll scout ahead." He nudged the horse with his heels, and it picked up speed. They watched him for a few minutes until the road took him over a small hill.

Darien held up his hand for the soldiers behind him and slowed their pace. If there was trouble ahead, he didn't want to rush into it.

Half an hour later, Colonel Oliver returned. He looked frazzled. As he brought his horse to a stop in front of Darien, he reported, "Palatians. They have taken Kellen."

"No! Kellen is a good two miles inside Marus land!" Darien said.

"They're a brazen bunch," agreed Colonel Oliver. "Let's attack immediately!"

"Not so fast," Darien insisted. "Not until we have a plan." He quickly looked around, then pointed to a hill in the distance. "Let's camp there until we decide what to do."

The debate among Darien and his officers on the hilltop

went on for an hour. Some of them said there was little they could do to help the people of Kellen since they had only sidearms, a few rifles, and their swords. Others said it was the king's responsibility to save Kellen, not theirs. He'd learn of the Palatian attack soon enough and would have to respond, they reasoned. Colonel Oliver felt strongly that they should attack the Palatians and drive them from Kellen—it was their duty as Marutians—but he confessed that he didn't know how.

Darien listened to the debate, sitting with his hands folded under his chin. Apart from a question or two, he didn't contribute to their arguing. From the top of the hill, he looked out across the flat green fields and to the Valley of the Rocks far beyond. "Majestic," he said.

The debate ceased as his officers turned to him. "What did you say?" they asked.

"Majestic," he repeated. "Look at the beauty of this land. It speaks of the glory of the Unseen One."

"Haven't you been listening to us, General?" an officer with a wolflike face asked irritably.

Darien stood up and walked over to Kyle and Anna, who'd been watching the debate with undisguised boredom. They would have entertained themselves with something else or rested from the journey, but Darien had asked them to stay nearby. They were about to understand why.

"What do you think, Kyle?" Darien asked.

Kyle was shocked to be put on the spot like that. He blushed, then stammered, "What do I think?"

"You're my guardian angel," Darien said with a smile. "Would I be in danger if I attacked the Palatians?"

Kyle struggled with his answer. He wanted to impress Darien and his officers with his cleverness and insight. But the truth was nothing in his gut instinct helped him one way or the other. However it was that he knew when Darien was in danger, he couldn't manufacture the feeling or predict when it would come. Finally, he shrugged and answered, "I don't know, General."

A few of the officers chuckled. Darien ignored them. "Anna?" he asked.

"Yes, sir?"

"You have been taught by the Old Judge and Sister Leona. You, better than most of us, know the ancient ways."

"I don't know that much," Anna said, also embarrassed about being made the center of attention.

Darien leaned close to her and said gently, "Yes, you do. You see what we cannot see, then speak what we can't hear."

She searched Darien's face and watched as it suddenly transformed from the confident face she saw now into a dirt-smudged, sweaty, and weary face in her dream. "Darien—" she began to say, but he turned away from her. He was in front of a roomful of people where he raised a chalice and said, "May the Unseen One receive glory from our victory!"

Standing in the corner of the room was a group of scowling soldiers—Anna didn't recognize their uniforms but guessed they must be Palatians. Next to them, standing like a proud guard, was the mayor of Kellen, a grin stretched across his chubby face. How she knew who he was, Anna couldn't say. But she recognized him as surely as if she'd seen him a dozen times.

"To the Unseen One!" everyone shouted as they drank from their cups.

Darien turned back to Anna. His face was no longer smudged or tired. He looked as he had before. "Anna?" he said.

Anna blinked a couple of times. The room, the people, and the Palatian soldiers were gone. She was back on the hill-top. "What?" she asked.

"Will you tell us what the Unseen One wants us to do?"

"You'll win," she responded. "You'll save Kellen and win."

Darien smiled and told her, "Thank you."

Anna sat back and rubbed her burning eyes.

Addressing his officers, Darien said, "All right, we'll attack the Palatians."

"No!" the officer with the wolflike face said. "It'll be a slaughter! We can't go against them with the weapons or men we have."

"The Unseen One goes with us."

"Because this *girl* said so?"

Darien looked at his officer with a determined expression. "She is a voice," he said. "We will have victory because of the Unseen One."

Colonel Oliver stood up. "You heard the general! Now let's get everyone ready!" he ordered.

After Darien and his officers walked away, Kyle asked Anna, "How did you do that?"

Anna slowly shook her head, a helpless look on her face. "I don't know how it happens. How do you know when Darien is in danger? It just happens, right? It's the Unseen One who does it."

"But you're sure we'll win?"

"We'll win."

Kellen was a walled town, fortresslike in appearance, with a large gate that served as its only formal entrance. But it also had smaller entry points along the seemingly endless circular wall for bringing in livestock and getting rid of rubbish. General Darien disguised a dozen of his men as traders and shepherds, then sent them in one and two at a time to position themselves at those entrances. The Palatians would be looking for a large army headed by the king of Marus, Darien knew. They wouldn't be on the lookout for stealth fighters.

The Palatian officers had taken over the mayor's offices and residence. The remaining Palatians—almost 1,000 in all—camped in the open spaces around the town. The citizens of Kellen were beaten into submission by the Palatians, then told to go about their business as usual and be ready to serve the Palatians as needed.

On Darien's signal, after the sun had gone down, the rest of the men casually entered the city and began to quietly capture or kill the soldiers who'd been put on guard duty.

While his disguised men carefully dispatched pockets of Palatian soldiers, Darien and Kyle walked past the guards at the front gate (they had been captured and replaced by Colonel Oliver and other Marutian soldiers). They made their way to the center of the city. Kyle was dressed in his normal clothes, while Darien was dressed in his general's uniform.

"I sure hope this works," Kyle whispered once they were positioned in the middle of the main marketplace. Torches blazed on all sides, casting an eerie yellow glow on the two of them. As a first impression, Kyle thought Kellen looked like a cross between a Western town (like Dodge City) and a village from Robin Hood's days.

Darien winked at Kyle, then shouted, "I am Darien! Come and take me!"

He had to shout it a few times before the Palatians could

be stirred to respond. As they surrounded him, Darien crouched down and began to jump around like a monkey, making screeching and hooting noises.

A Palatian officer broke through the circle of soldiers. He had dark, slicked-back hair and a pointed beard. "What's going on here?" he demanded.

Kyle rushed forward to him. "Please, sir, I found this man wandering in the forest," he said. "He kept screaming that he was General Darien. I brought him here for the reward you Palatians said you'd give for handing him over."

On hearing his name, Darien screeched even louder: "Darien! Darien!" He made faces at the soldiers, tugged at their shirts, and even tried to climb on the shoulders of a guard.

"I don't have time for madmen," the officer said, clearly not believing what he was seeing.

"Mad?" Darien cried. "Me mad? Mad me? I am Darien! Take me to your leader!"

"My leaders are busy," the officer growled. "Now go away."

Darien wouldn't be so easily brushed aside. He howled like a dog, then screeched and danced like a monkey. "Take me to your leader!" he yelled over and over.

Kyle grabbed the officer's sleeve and asked, "If this man is really Darien, what'll your bosses say if you let him go?"

That stopped the officer.

"Take us to your general," Kyle said. "Let's talk business."

The officer signaled for two of his men to help lead Darien to the mayor's office.

General Gaiman, head of that particular Palatian regiment, wasn't pleased to see his officer, Darien, or Kyle. He frowned wearily, the deep lines on his dark forehead bunching up over his nose. "He looks like Darien, but he's obviously mad as a hatter," he concluded.

Darien was racing around the room, knocking things off the desk and walls.

"Get rid of him," General Gaiman said.

"How?" the pointy-bearded officer asked.

"Throw him back outside the gate or lock him up—I don't care. I'm more concerned about Lawrence's army, which will likely show up any time now."

The officer sighed, then gestured for two guards to take Darien back out.

"What about my reward?" Kyle complained.

"Your reward is that I'll let you go free rather than kill you," the general said. "Now get out."

At the doorway, Kyle and Darien exchanged a quick look and then sprang into action. Darien pushed the two guards into the hall and closed the door on them. Kyle pulled out a small pistol he had tucked under his shirt and fired it at the front window. The sound of the shot and the breaking glass were the signal for Darien's men to attack throughout the town.

In one fast motion, Darien deftly swung around, grabbed a large marble bust from a nearby pedestal, and brought it crashing against the officer's head. General Gaiman dashed to the desk, where a pistol sat in a holster hanging from the chair. But Kyle, who was closer, reached it before him and snatched it up.

"Give me that!" the general snapped.

Kyle threw the pistol to Darien, who caught it with one hand and then pointed the muzzle at the general. He smiled. "Now sit down so we can go over your terms of surrender," he ordered.

Within two hours, Kellen was once again a Marutian

town. While many Palatians were wounded, killed, or had fled from the town, not a single member of Darien's army was hurt.

In a banquet room at Kellen's largest (and only) hotel, Darien raised a toast to the Unseen One and the victory He'd given them. The Palatian officers scowled, the mayor of Kellen grinned a chubby grin—and Anna smiled because the scene was exactly as she remembered it.

CHAPTER 13

The stranger arrived at Kellen first thing the next morning. He came on horseback and wore a long cloak and a wrap that hid his face and protected it from the sun. Darien's guards at the front gate let him through but used the phone in the guardhouse to alert Darien that the stranger was coming. Darien was having breakfast with some of his officers, along with Anna and Kyle, at the Kellen Hotel's restaurant.

When told that the stranger had reached the front of the hotel, Darien threw his napkin onto his plate and got up. He walked from the restaurant, through the plush lobby, and out onto the front sidewalk just as the stranger dismounted. Kyle felt nothing in his stomach to alert him to any danger. Anna was silent.

"Darien!" the stranger said warmly and pulled the wrap from his face.

"George!" said Darien happily. The two men shook hands, embraced, then went back into the hotel. Darien offered the prince some breakfast.

"I'm afraid I don't have much time," George said. He looked older than Kyle remembered. Could he have aged so much in just a few days?

Darien sipped some coffee. "Then tell me what you're doing here," he said.

"The king knows you're here," George answered. "He's been tracking you ever since you left your parents. In fact, word is getting around the entire country about the battle with the Palatians."

"How could they know so fast?" Darien asked, surprised.

"The way they know everything faster than we expect," George replied. "My father and General Liddell contacted the newspapers."

"To what purpose?"

"They reported that you came here to negotiate with the Palatians, but a loyal royal regiment attacked and drove the Palatians away. The *Sarum Herald* is saying that my father and General Liddell will come to secure the town and capture you for your treason."

Darien couldn't believe what he was hearing. He fumed, "How could they spread such lies and still call themselves honorable men?"

"They dispensed with calling themselves honorable men a long time ago. My father is truly insane. I see that now." George hesitated, then added, "I've come to affirm my allegiance to you and your future kingship—and to warn you that you'll be grossly outnumbered when my father's troops arrive."

"Does the king know you're here?" Darien asked.

"No. He left Sarum without asking where I was or where I would be going. I'm not sure he trusts me anymore. He does things without consulting me."

"Like attack Sister Leona and the women at the convent?"

George went pale. "That wasn't my father's doing," he insisted. "He may be insane, but he's no barbarian."

Darien glanced over at Anna, who was nibbling on a crescent roll. "I know otherwise," he said grimly. "The attack was his idea."

George looked as though he might be sick—or argue—or both. But he didn't.

"Stay with us, George," Darien urged. "Don't go back to him."

"I . . . must," George said, grieved. "While he lives he's still my father and my king, and I have to support him."

"In everything?"

George shook his head. "Not everything. But my remaining with him will be useful to you. I can send you information about his plans, to the best of my ability."

Darien thought it over, then reluctantly agreed. "All right," he said, "but please be careful, George. And know this: If and when I am king, you will rule with me. That I promise."

"Ruin," Anna suddenly said. She had a distant look on her face.

"What?" Darien asked.

"I see ruin. A terrible battle. The king and his family will not survive against you."

"Against *me*? I will not fight the king—or his family."

"I see many wounds and blood and . . ." Anna suddenly gasped. She dropped her roll without seeming to notice. In a different tone she said, "Darien, the people of Kellen will hand you over to the king."

"Will they?"

The mayor, who sat eating at a nearby table, blustered, "Hand our champion over to the king? Never! What kind of thing is that to say?"

Anna said plainly, "The king will surround the city and

demand that they deliver you. They will. You must leave Kellen now."

"Thank you, Anna," Darien said.

Anna's eyes cleared, and she turned red to see everyone staring at her. "What's wrong?" she asked.

"We're leaving," Darien announced and stood up.

———— ⚜ ————

Prince George left and, within an hour, Darien's men were mobilized to leave Kellen. The mayor was insistent to the last minute that Darien could stay. Darien said he appreciated his offer but felt it would be better for all if they left.

As they rode out of town, Anna looked back at the mayor, who stood waving at the front gate like a bowling ball over-dressed in a coat and vest, a gold watch chain linked from his vest button to a small pocket on the side. In her mind's eye, Anna saw that the watch had belonged to someone close to the king. Just as the watch was in the mayor's pocket, so was the mayor in the king's pocket. He'd been reporting to the king's spies everything that had happened.

That meant the king and his army were closer than any of them realized. Anna saw them on the horizon as clearly as if they'd really been there.

"We have to hurry up," she told Darien.

Darien didn't question or argue with her statement. He simply ordered everyone to pick up their pace.

———— ⚜ ————

The Valley of the Rocks was well named. It was mostly desert, with only spots of vegetation near what was left of a dying river. The rest of it was dirt and tumbleweeds. The rocks, which rose canyonlike on two sides, were a beautiful reddish pink—Kyle and Anna had no idea what they were called—and jutted up in formations that could easily be seen as faces or figurines. They surrounded Darien's army on all sides.

"We'll have to find good hiding places or we'll be surrounded by more than just rocks," Darien said. He gave instructions for the 100 of them to split up into four groups of 25 and then camp at strategic places around the valley.

"But if we split up," Colonel Oliver observed, "the king will have a better chance of defeating us."

"But if we stay together, he'll have a better chance of finding us," Darien countered. "It's easier to hide small groups of 25 than a whole army of 100."

"But General—"

Darien held up his hand. "I know it's a gamble. And unless Anna has words of wisdom for us, I think it's the best thing for us to do."

Anna didn't have any words of wisdom. She closed her eyes, but no dreams or visions came.

Darien and his group of 25, including Kyle and Anna, slowly wove their way through the rocks on the north side of the valley. It was a tortuous climb for both people and horses. They went up and up until they found a large cleft in one of the rocks that would shelter them all. It curved into a deep cave where they had plenty of room. It also afforded them a vantage point to the valley in all directions. Darien was troubled only by the existence of a ridge above them, one that might give the king's army a chance to trap him. But he had to take a chance. His people were exhausted, and they were running out of places to hide.

While they set up camp, Kyle got a sick feeling in the pit

of his stomach. He looked around quickly to see what was causing it. The soldiers were busy arranging their provisions or unpacking their knapsacks. Darien sat quietly in the corner. He was either thinking or praying—or both. Still, the sick feeling grew worse.

Kyle walked over to Darien. "I'm sorry to bother you," he started to say. But just then, a shot rang out. The entire squad drew their pistols and swords instantaneously. Darien leaped to his feet and went to the edge of the cave.

"Surrender now and we may be merciful!" someone shouted from afar, the voice bouncing and echoing around the rock walls. Darien recognized the voice. It was General Liddell.

"I'll check their position," a young soldier said. Before Darien could stop him, he had crept out of the cave and raced to a rock farther out in the open. He looked around, then signaled to Darien that the king's army was situated in four places on the long ridge above them. Darien cursed himself for not paying closer attention to his instincts. They were trapped.

"Yes, trapped!" General Liddell called out as if he knew what the signals meant. "We've been watching you for hours. Did you think we were so foolish as to not anticipate that you'd come to the Valley of the Rocks to hide? We've been hiding here since you defeated the Palatians at Kellen last night. The king is here. He wants desperately to see you."

"It's true, my son!" the king shouted. "Come! Embrace me!"

Darien's face was expressionless. He said nothing.

General Liddell then said, "To demonstrate how effectively you are trapped . . ."

Another shot rang out, and the young scout suddenly

clutched his chest and fell behind the rock he mistakenly thought was protecting him.

"No!" Darien cried out, and he would've run to the young man if he hadn't been grabbed by some of his other soldiers.

"What are we going to do?" one of them asked.

"I'm going to surrender myself to them," Darien replied quickly.

Another soldier immediately protested, "No! You can't! They'll kill you!"

"Better for me to take that chance than for everyone here to die in this trap."

"Well?" General Liddell shouted.

Another soldier stepped forward. "Maybe Colonel Oliver and the others will see what's happening and rescue us."

"If *they* haven't already been captured," Darien reminded him. "Though, if George was right, we're so outnumbered that they couldn't do us much good anyway."

"But you're our future king!" the first soldier said. "If you die, the rest of us will die anyway for having joined you."

"Better to die fighting!" a third soldier added.

"If I'm to be your future king, I'm in the hands of the Unseen One anyway," Darien said. "He will do with me whatever He wills, whether I stay here or go."

With the mention of the Unseen One, Darien looked over at Anna. She sat on a rock nearby and trembled. Her eyes filled with tears. The Unseen One hadn't given her any sort of dream or vision about what they should do. She shook her head and slumped sadly.

The discussion continued for a few more minutes, the soldiers arguing that surely the Unseen One wouldn't have brought them this far only to have Darien "throw his life away" now. Finally, Darien beckoned everyone to kneel. "A moment of silent prayer," he said.

Five minutes later, he stood up. "I will go," he said and pushed through his soldiers, ignoring their protests. He went to the mouth of the cave. Taking a deep breath, he stepped out into the open. Darien didn't know what he expected. But he certainly didn't expect *nothing* to happen. Scanning the ridges above, he was surprised to see that they were empty. He suspected that General Liddell's soldiers were simply out of view.

"Hello?" he called out. He thought someone—General Liddell or the king himself—would appear. He got no response, not even sniper fire.

He ventured farther out, past the body of the dead scout. "All right, General, you win," he shouted. "Tell the king I will surrender myself—provided you let my men go!"

General Liddell didn't respond. No one did. Again, nothing happened.

The feeling in the pit of Kyle's stomach went away. "General?" he called out.

Darien waved him back. "Hello?" he shouted to the valley. "Are you playing games with me?" No one answered. Darien moved farther out and climbed up on a rock. He waved. "Hello? Is anybody out there?" Shielding his eyes from the sun, he scanned the valley and the rock walls. He looked back at the cave and shrugged.

Kyle, Anna, and the soldiers wandered out into the open.

Darien stepped down from the rock. "I don't understand this at all," he said.

Small pebbles fell at their feet. They all looked up in time to see Colonel Oliver scurrying down across the rocks toward them. "It's unbelievable!" he said breathlessly as he got closer. "Unbelievable!"

"Slow down, Colonel," Darien ordered.

The colonel panted but smiled as he reported, "We were surrounded. On all sides. No chance of escape. They had us, General."

"I know all that," Darien said. "But why haven't they captured us? Where are they?"

"They left."

"Left! They had us where they wanted us, and they simply up and left?"

"Yes! We watched them leave! They were poised to attack us, and then they suddenly retreated. I've never seen an army move so fast."

"But why?"

Colonel Oliver eyed them for dramatic effect. His red complexion was alight. "We picked up on our shortwave wireless the very thing that *they* picked up. A distress call. The Palatians have attacked Furnchance, just to the south. A massive Palatian army. Retaliation for your victory in Kellen, probably. There was no time to lose. They couldn't capture you *and* fight the Palatians, so the king and General Liddell left! It was that simple." Colonel Oliver was laughing now.

Darien watched him, the news still slowly sinking in.

Colonel Oliver clapped him on the back. "You, my dear general, were saved from your worst enemies *by* your worst enemies!"

With that, they all began to laugh. They laughed long and hard—not the laugh of those who were amused but of those who felt a great sense of relief.

The battle of Furnchance was no small skirmish. It marked the beginning of a war between Marus and Palatia. The Palatians, a civilization founded on principles of conquest and domination, unleashed everything they had in the southern part of Marus. King Lawrence, General Liddell, and their best advisers were busy for weeks keeping the Palatians on their own side of the border. No one had time to think about Darien or where he and his men had gone.

They had, in fact, hidden in the hills of the Territory of Peace, in the far north of Marus where Darien had helped to thwart an attack from the Adrians and was nearly assassinated by one of General Liddell's men. (There was no doubt about it now.)

A network of communication developed throughout the country as Darien's secret got around. Anyone who had ever been abused or victimized by King Lawrence joined Darien's side. Some stayed in their own towns and contributed money or food to Darien's men. Others actually traveled to the Territory of Peace, where they pledged themselves to help Darien in any way they could. Kyle and Anna took on simple duties and responsibilities to help around the camp, all the while wondering and worrying about their family and friends back in their own world. When could they go back? In time, they began to second-guess themselves. Did they really *want* to go back?

"Of course we do!" Anna said one afternoon as they were picking vegetables from a makeshift garden. "We have to go back!"

"Don't you like it here?" Kyle asked.

"Yes! But that's not the point. Mom and Dad will be worried about us. And who knows what this has done to poor Grandma and Grandpa? We've been gone for weeks!"

Kyle wiped a spot of dirt from his sister's chin. "But I like being a helper to the future king of Marus," he said honestly. "It'll be so boring to go back to our world and school and normal things and be . . . just *me* again."

"But we're chosen by the Unseen One," Anna replied. "Aren't we chosen there as well as here?"

"I hope so, but it won't be the same," Kyle observed sadly.

Anna knew he was right. Somehow—though she didn't understand how—she realized that whatever power she had as a voice and whatever it was that made Kyle a protector, those gifts would be gone if the two of them left Marus. She wondered then, as later, if God would give them different kinds of gifts or choose them for different tasks in *their* world. What had her grandparents said about it? That all believers were called to serve Him. But Kyle was right. It wouldn't be the same.

She sighed. "But we still have to go back," she insisted. "I'm going to ask Darien about it at dinner tonight. I'm going to ask him to let us go back to the Old Judge and see how we can get home."

True to her word, Anna sat down next to Darien near the fire where dinner was prepared. Kyle sat on his other side. They both noticed that Darien looked worried and preoccupied.

"Have you seen anything lately?" Darien asked Anna before she could speak.

Anna had to admit that she hadn't. Occasionally she had dreams of the king in battle against the Palatians, but they were fuzzy, unspecific dreams, like old newsreels of somebody else's war somewhere. It had been awhile since she'd had the kinds of visions and dreams that had helped them.

"The Unseen One has been so quiet," Darien said. A twinge of sadness in his voice alarmed Anna and Kyle. "It's as if He is allowing His voice to . . . to . . ." He stopped. A tear slid down his cheek.

"What's wrong, Darien?" asked Anna anxiously.

"The Old Judge is dead."

"No . . ." Kyle said.

"What?" Anna was stunned.

"He died in his sleep this morning. The Unseen One has taken him away."

Kyle stared into the fire. He didn't know what to feel.

Anna began to cry. "But he *can't* die!" she insisted. "He can't *ever* die!"

Darien pulled her close with one arm, then wrapped another around Kyle. "Yes," he agreed, "he should have lived forever."

They all wept together.

Against the advice of his officers, Darien decided to disguise himself and take a train to Hailsham for the Old Judge's funeral. He explained to them that it was the least he could do after all the Old Judge had done for him. Colonel Oliver insisted on going along. So did Kyle and Anna. They were also determined to pay their last respects to the old prophet. Darien's other officers harrumphed and argued with them up to the very last minute.

By now, Darien was hard to recognize. He hadn't shaved since the narrow escape at the Valley of the Rocks and had a full beard and mustache. His curly hair also had streaks of gray in it. With his country-folk clothes and hat, he could have been anyone. Few would've guessed that he was the great General Darien.

The small party booked a first-class compartment on a train from Krawley and traveled without incident south toward Hailsham. They knew they were scheduled to stop in the main terminal in Sarum, but they didn't worry since the king was reported to be with General Liddell at Kellen. Kellen had become an important headquarters for the king and his leaders since the war with Palatia had begun. Besides, no one thought much about Darien anymore. The war was on everyone's minds, first and foremost.

As the train pulled into the Sarum station, Darien looked wistfully at the capital city. "I wonder if I will ever be able to return here," he said softly. Considering he was a die-hard country boy, he was surprised to find that he'd fallen in love with the city.

"You're going to be king here!" Colonel Oliver insisted with feeling.

"I wonder . . ." Darien said.

Anna opened her mouth to assure him that he would be king. There were few things on earth of which she could be absolutely certain, but Darien's kingship was one of them. Something prompted her to keep silent, however. Somehow she knew that Darien would have to see—and believe—for himself.

The train to Hailsham sat at the station longer than they had expected. Five minutes, ten minutes, then half an hour went by. The train didn't move. Even the people on the platform seemed to thin out until it was virtually empty. Colonel Oliver got nervous and went into the hall to ask a steward what the holdup was. When the colonel returned a few minutes later, he was white as a ghost.

Kyle felt that sick feeling again in his stomach.

"It's the king," Colonel Oliver said. "He's getting on the train!"

"What train?" Darien asked. "He has his own train, and it's in Kellen, where *he's* supposed to be."

Colonel Oliver gestured wildly as he explained, "He's not in Kellen, he's *here*. And his train is having mechanical problems, so he's getting on *this* train. He's going to Hailsham for the Old Judge's funeral!"

Darien put a hand over his mouth to keep from laughing.

"You think this is funny, General?" Colonel Oliver asked indignantly. "They're putting him in the carriage ahead of us. He has a compartment *right in front of us.* I think we should get off now, while we can."

"And I think we should go up and say hello."

"This isn't amusing."

"Sit down, Colonel. If we make a run for it now, they'll suspect us. Let's just stick to our plan, all right? The king isn't a politician. He won't venture back here to shake our hands or ask how our families are. He'll stay in his carriage, and we'll stay in ours."

Colonel Oliver looked at him skeptically. "And when we get to Hailsham?"

Darien sat back casually. "We'll get off the train with the hundreds of other people who are on it and lose ourselves in the crowd. Don't panic."

"Panic? Who's panicked?" the colonel said as he wiped beads of sweat from his freckled forehead.

With a jolt, the train suddenly began to move from the station. Within a few minutes it was going full speed.

"Half an hour is all it should take," said Darien. "They won't make any more stops with the king on board." He had a mischievous look on his face. A smile crept onto his lips. "Maybe I *should* go say hello to the king."

"What?" Colonel Oliver cried, exasperated.

"It's dangerous," Kyle warned, his stomach still churning.

"Just a quick little visit. Why not?" Darien said.

Anna shook her head silently, like a mother with a precocious child.

"You're going to kill him then?" Colonel Oliver asked.

"Kill him! He's the king," Darien said earnestly. "Chosen by the Unseen One. I won't raise my hand against him."

Colonel Oliver pointed a finger at him. "Well, if you're going to all the trouble of dropping in on him, I suspect you'll have to kill him as well. He's not going to give you a nice, big howdy-do and let you go."

"No, I suppose not," Darien admitted thoughtfully, then brightened again. "A quick peek won't hurt, though. I won't have to speak to him. You said his compartment is just ahead?"

"Yes, but—"

Before Colonel Oliver could say anything else, Darien was on his feet and opening the outside door to their compartment. Wind rushed in, nearly yanking the door from his hand. The inside door, the one that led into the carriage hall, rattled in its frame.

"How are you going to get there?" Colonel Oliver asked, his face the picture of worry.

"Plenty of rods and rails to hold on to," Darien said as he stepped halfway outside. The wind pounded against him, pressing his hair back and turning his shirt into a billowing sheet. "Each door has its own step. I'll simply pull myself from one to another until I find his compartment."

"And if someone reports you *before* you get to his compartment?"

"Then I'll jump off the train and meet you later in Hailsham."

"Oh, that's a comfort."

"It's something fun to do!" he said like a little boy. "I haven't had any fun since I got those Palatian medals. Bye!" He slipped out the door. They watched him as he clung to the side of the train like a spider, inching his way forward, swinging from one step to the next. The train went into a black tunnel, and when it emerged into the light again, Darien was gone.

"How's your stomach?" Colonel Oliver asked Kyle after a few minutes.

"I feel sick," Kyle said.

"So he's still in danger?"

"I guess so. But I can't be his guardian angel if he's going to do stuff like this."

Colonel Oliver nodded. "Agreed," he said. "He sometimes makes it difficult for all of us." The colonel paused, but it was clear he still had something on his mind. Finally he looked at Kyle and said, "When I first met you, I spoke harshly to you. I didn't trust you and suspected you were out to hurt General Darien. I was wrong, of course, and I want to apologize to you for thinking the worst." He reached out his hand, and Kyle shook it. "No hard feelings?"

"No hard feelings," Kyle said.

"Thank you."

Fifteen minutes later, Colonel Oliver was aggressively pacing their compartment, stopping only to peer out the window to see if Darien was coming back. Kyle squirmed in his seat, chewing fingernails that were already chewed to the nub, and Anna prayed that the Unseen One would be merciful even though Darien didn't deserve it.

Five minutes later, all three of them were pacing circles with Colonel Oliver. The steward announced that they would be arriving in Hailsham station in a minute.

"Do you think he jumped off the train?" Kyle asked.

"I have no idea," Colonel Oliver said, "but I could kill him myself for doing something like this."

The train began to slow as it approached Hailsham. Anna stood at the window and thought sadly about the Old Judge. She had hoped to see him again. Now she never would. Colonel Oliver and Kyle joined her at the window. Darien was still nowhere to be seen.

Just as the train came to a stop at the platform, the inside door of the compartment opened behind them. Darien stepped in from the hallway with a wry smile on his face. He was dressed in a steward's uniform and cap.

"I could make a living doing this," he said as he tossed the cap onto the sofa and began to unbutton the steward's vest. "The pay's rotten, but the tips are pretty good."

"Well, what happened?" they all demanded.

Darien put on a disappointed expression. "Sadly, the king was sleeping," he answered. "He didn't even wake up when I slipped into his compartment. I nearly tucked him in and kissed him on the forehead, he looked so sweet and innocent."

Colonel Oliver groaned.

Darien's expression changed to one of disapproval. "It's a terrible comment about the king's security when a man like me can get in to him like that. I should write to someone about it."

"I'm sure General Liddell would love to hear from you," Anna giggled.

"And so he shall! Imagine leaving the king to ride on a train with only a few guards around him. Just because he's battling the Palatians doesn't give him the excuse to—"

"So how did you get back?" Colonel Oliver interrupted.

"Easy. A steward knocked on the door and came in. The king told him to go away and rolled over. I quietly gave the steward a wad of money for his coat and hat and 10 minutes of silence. He accepted the offer. I came out and walked back here without any questions or problems." He glanced at his watch. "Though the 10 minutes are almost up, and that steward is going to have to explain why he's been sitting in the king's toilet while on duty."

"Let's get out of here," Colonel Oliver said and headed for the door.

"Good idea." Darien didn't move but fished in his pocket and pulled out a large gold medallion on a red ribbon. "Do you think the king will miss this? I took it as a memento of my visit."

Colonel Oliver went bug-eyed. "The king's medallion?" he said. "You stole the *king's medallion*?"

"It looked so pretty sitting there. How could I resist?"

"The king's medallion?" Kyle asked. "Is it important?"

"Oh, not at all," Colonel Oliver said sarcastically. "It's only the medallion the king is given at his coronation."

"He shouldn't have taken it off and left it lying around."

"I don't want to hear about it," Colonel Oliver said.

"I'll give it back to him one day."

Colonel Oliver waved him away. "Don't say another word."

When the crowd was at its peak on the platform, the four of them got off the train and seemed to disappear among the people. As they walked past the window of the king's carriage, they saw two stern-looking guards interrogating a steward.

CHAPTER

15

Anna had never been to a funeral before, at least not that she could recall. She'd gone to her grandfather's funeral as a baby, but she had no memory of it. This was the first time someone had died that Anna knew and, in her own way, loved.

The service for the Old Judge was held in an old church in Hailsham. The stone building was beautiful with its tower, pillars lining the inside, stained-glass windows, and smooth wooden pews. It reminded Anna of a miniature cathedral. She sat with Kyle, Darien, and Colonel Oliver in the back, among a crowd of local people. Dignitaries like the king and his guards sat in the front pew. The coffin was also in the front, by the altar, as a simple tribute to the man inside.

"But he isn't inside," the priest said in his eulogy. "This shallow encasement, this empty vessel, is not the man we loved and who loved us. He is somewhere else. The Old Judge is with the Unseen One, in the paradise created for all those who believe in Him."

Anna squeezed her eyes closed, not to ward off any tears but in the strong desire to "see" the Old Judge. She wanted a vision of him now, in that paradise. "Just let me see a little bit of it," Anna prayed. But nothing came except black and orange circles as her eyes readjusted to the light.

The service was over in 20 minutes. A line of mourners formed to pray beside the coffin or to touch it, but the top was closed and there was no final look at the man who'd been the Unseen One's voice for so many years.

"I want to see his cottage one more time," Anna pleaded. "Please."

Darien saw no reason not to go, so the four of them sneaked out the back door of the church and stayed off the beaten path to get there. If they had gone on the main road, they would have seen the large touring car waiting there, not far from the cottage. As it was, they walked up along the rear side, past the vegetable garden, and slipped in the small door that led into the kitchen. They crept in—and then stopped suddenly. The king stood alone in the middle of the living room.

Darien felt quickly for the pistol tucked into his trousers. Colonel Oliver put his hand on the hilt of his dagger. Anna and Kyle hung back a few steps, just in case something happened. Strangely, though, Kyle did not feel anything resembling a sense of danger.

The king didn't react to their arrival. He merely looked at them with red-rimmed eyes sunk into a deeply lined face. He looked so much older than the last time they'd seen him. He coughed wearily and said, "I thought I saw you in the back of the church."

"You did, Your Highness," Darien replied. "We didn't want to miss our last good-byes to the Old Judge."

The king waved his hand toward the room and continued, "I can't believe he's gone. It doesn't seem possible."

"I know what you mean, sire."

"It's *all* gone, isn't it? The days pass so quickly, and then . . ." He didn't finish the thought but looked at them, anguished.

They waited.

He sighed deeply. "And then come the days when you no longer know your friends from your enemies."

Darien stepped forward and said softly, "You have no enemies here, my king."

"Don't I?"

"No, sire." Darien was only a foot or two away from the king. "Listen no longer to those who whisper evil in your ear. Ignore the voices who say that I mean to do you harm. They are liars. You have been like a father to me. Would I turn my hand against you?"

"Others have."

"But I have not." Darien pulled the king's medallion from his pocket and held it up. The gold seemed to glow artificially in the shadow of the cottage.

The king instinctively put a hand to his chest, as if feeling to be sure the medallion wasn't there. "My medallion!" he exclaimed.

"It was within my power to take your life, just as I took this medallion," Darien said. "But I didn't. You are the chosen one, and I would be in defiance of the Unseen One to raise my hand against you." He handed the medallion to the king. The king took it with shaking hands. Darien continued, "I have done you no wrong, my king. Nor will I. May the Unseen One vindicate me in your eyes."

The king lowered his head. Then his shoulders began to shake as he started to weep, his whole body joining in. He grabbed Darien and cried out, "Darien, my son! What is this madness that afflicts me? How could I ever believe that you would hurt me?"

Darien held the king close. They both wept for several minutes.

The guards who'd been waiting by the touring car came to

the door and knocked. "Sire? Are you all right?" they asked. "We must return to Sarum now. General Liddell will be calling."

"Yes, yes," the king said impatiently. He gazed into Darien's face, touched the side of it softly, and told him, "The Old Judge was right. There is no doubt that you will be king. I pray only that you'll find it in your heart to have more mercy on me and my family than I did on you and yours. Good-bye, my son."

With that, the king turned away and left. He yelled at the guards as they walked to the car, as if they'd done something terribly wrong. "Just take me back to the station!" he concluded.

Darien slumped into a chair—the Old Judge's favorite— next to the cold fireplace. A chill swept through the room, and Anna thought then that the cottage would never be warm again.

<hr/>

The four of them spent the night at an inn halfway between Hailsham and Sarum, and then they caught the first train back to Krawley the next morning. Anna and Kyle spent most of the trip in silence, watching the rolling fields and thick forests wash past like gentle waves of green. Apart from the sadness of losing the Old Judge, the question that dominated their thinking was this: *How are we going to get home?* If the Old Judge was the only one who knew, they were now stuck.

Darien and Colonel Oliver spent the trip discussing plans for their future. "You don't believe King Lawrence will simply sit back and allow you to become the new king, do you?" Colonel Oliver asked.

"No," Darien said with a sigh. "His grief and remorse at the cottage were genuine enough, but once he returns to the splendor of his palace and the great power and the servants waiting on him hand and foot, he'll change his mind. He *likes* being the king and wants to keep it that way."

"So where do we go from here?"

Darien rubbed his hand over his beard. "I think we should keep on as we have."

Colonel Oliver wasn't satisfied. "But we've grown so much," he pointed out. "We have over 500 people in our group now. And the men are getting restless. It's driving them crazy sitting in the Territory of Peace while every fighting man is at war with the Palatians."

"What do they want to do?"

"Fight the Palatians, of course."

"I wish we could," Darien said ruefully. "But for us to openly join the war would invite the king to murder us on the battlefield and then blame the Palatians. No, it's too risky."

"There must be *something* we can do!" Colonel Oliver growled, frustrated.

Darien leaned toward the colonel. "There is," he affirmed. "We must pray. Then maybe an answer will present itself."

When they stepped onto the platform at the station in Krawley, Colonel Henri, one of Darien's officers, greeted them. "Welcome back," he said, then led them aside, close to the stationmaster's office. "A baron from Adria has come to meet with you. He and his servants waited for you all day yesterday. He said they wouldn't leave until they had a chance to talk to you."

"Where are they now?" Darien asked.

"The Lion's Head Pub in the center of town," Colonel Henri answered.

"Are they safe?" Colonel Oliver asked. "I wouldn't put it past our king to hire Adrians to kill us."

Colonel Henri nodded. "We searched them thoroughly. They're unarmed except for weapons they keep on their horses for when they travel. They won't be near their horses when they meet you."

"Then I suppose I should talk to them," said Darien.

"What about the kids?" Colonel Henri asked. "Do you want me to take them back to our camp?"

Darien didn't need to think about it. "Of course not," he replied. "I wouldn't dare meet the baron without my prophet and my guardian angel."

They walked straight to the Lion's Head Pub and went inside. Like most pubs, it was decorated in dark paneling, dark furniture, and dark paintings. Even the light through the windows seemed dark. The baron, who couldn't have been missed in any circumstance, was a big, ostentatious man dressed in a large cloak laced with orange fur. He had a thick, heavy brow that kept his eyes in constant shadow and round, wobbly jowls that shook when he laughed. His mannerisms, even before he spoke, included flamboyant gestures with his hands and an affected accent that no nation would want as its own. Most noticeable was his size. He stood up to receive them, and Anna guessed he was at least six-foot-five. His two guards, who were also tall, looked like dwarves next to their boss.

"I wonder why he even *needs* guards," Kyle said softly to Anna as they crossed the room.

"Thank you for meeting with me. I am Baron Orkzy," the man said in a thunderous voice.

"I knew who you were instantly," Darien said. "Your reputation is known by everyone."

"You're too kind."

Kyle noticed that Darien didn't say exactly what sort of reputation the baron had.

Darien introduced everyone. The baron shook hands, his bearlike paw swallowing each of theirs, then invited them to sit down at the table with him.

"We need to discuss a matter of business," the baron said once they were comfortable. "As you know, I'm a man with many friends and many enemies. My wealth intimidates some, and my work in—shall we say, *negotiations*—with certain parties annoys others."

"In other words, there are people who hate you because you'll do anything for money," Darien said flatly.

The baron laughed, and his jowls shook. "Yes! Yes! Precisely! Straight to the point. Score one for you, General."

"What can I do for you?" Darien asked.

"I want to hire you."

"I beg your pardon?"

The baron rested his elbows on the table. It tilted beneath the weight. He feigned a great weariness and said, "The war between your country and the Palatians is a nasty affair. Frankly, I don't feel safe anymore. Because of my past dealings with the Palatians, I'm afraid your people—or your allies—may attack me. Because of my past dealings with the Marutians, I'm afraid the Palatians and *their* allies will attack."

"Why come to me? Adrians are known for their love of war. It seems like there are plenty of tribes around to protect you."

"And that is where you've hit the nail directly on the head. My country has been torn apart by petty differences for years. Few of the leaders will stop bickering long enough to see the bigger picture. They're barbarians, mostly. I don't trust a single one of them." He placed his hand against his forehead melodramatically. "Alas, I am a man without a country. Much like you, I dare say."

"I understand," replied Darien dryly.

"I want to hire you and your *entourage* to be my body-guards. I want you to help me to protect my interests. You'll be my own personal army, as such. In exchange, you'll be well looked after. Your people will even have better accommodations than you have here. Imagine living in houses rather than tents on a hillside. Gas, electricity, plumbing, proper sewage . . ." The baron lifted an eyebrow coaxingly.

Darien's tone and expression betrayed no answer one way or the other. He said simply, "I'll have to give it some thought, Baron."

"Yes, yes. Consult with your officers."

"Can we meet again tomorrow morning?"

"I'd be delighted," the baron said with a flourish of his hand. He pulled a handkerchief from his sleeve and dabbed the side of his nose. He waved the handkerchief at them as they stood up and left. "Until tomorrow!"

As they walked out of the pub, Darien said to Colonel Oliver, "Check the grapevine and find out what he's really up to."

"Yes, sir," the colonel replied.

"Don't you trust him?" Kyle asked.

"Baron Orkzy is a mercenary who'll greet you with one hand and stab you in the back with the other," Darien said.

"Then why are you going to meet with him again?" asked Anna.

"Because it's possible that we can suit our own purposes while trying to suit his."

That evening at the camp, Anna and Kyle were summoned to Darien's tent. Just as they arrived, Colonel Oliver brought in a man who looked surprisingly like a rat. He had a pointed nose, small teeth, and whiskers that spread out from his face like fur. He even held his hands in front of him like a rat when it's on its hind legs, looking for food. And he was called, appropriately enough, the Rat.

"Sit down," Darien said.

"I'd rather stand, if you don't mind," the Rat replied. "I get fidgety sitting down."

"The Rat has some useful information for us," Colonel Oliver explained.

Darien smiled graciously. "We've paid well for it, I assume?"

The Rat's head jerked up and down quickly. "Oh yes," he said. "The general always pays well. I hope to honor you with my information in return."

"Then tell us what you know."

"I have it from reliable sources that the baron's offer to you is a good one," the Rat began, his nose twitching. "He can and will provide you with an entire town in which to live. It's called Lizah, just inside the Adrian border. What he wants from you in return is to see that he is kept safe and that some of his 'product' gets safely to market."

"What product?" Darien asked suspiciously.

The Rat smiled, his lips turning into a giant U. "Ah, this is where it gets most interesting. The baron is a partner in a firm that has created the parts for a new long-range cannon. It shoots farther than anything in existence—up to 300 yards farther. But the Adrians don't have the internal stability or the factories to build the cannons themselves. That's why the parts must be delivered."

"Delivered where?" asked Darien.

"Monrovia."

Darien and Colonel Oliver glanced at each other. "Monrovia?" the colonel asked.

"Yes. They assemble the baron's cannon parts with their own."

Colonel Oliver pressed on. "Why is Monrovia interested in this cannon? They're not at war with anyone."

"They're not at war now, but they might be one day." The Rat's eyes flickered.

"You know something else," Darien said. "Out with it."

"I have it from another good source that the Monrovians are going to sell the assembled cannons to the Palatians."

"I see."

Colonel Oliver stood up and began to pace. "With that kind of firepower, the Palatians could defeat our armies in a matter of weeks," he observed.

The Rat sniffed. "In exchange for the cannons, the Palatians will give the Monrovians part of your territories."

"Carve us up like a Christmas goose," the colonel said. "Is that what they have in mind?"

"Likely."

Darien mused, "Does the baron know about this?"

"I can't say for sure. Though there is little that the baron doesn't know."

"Is it possible that he wants me to be his bodyguard to get me out of the way?" asked Darien. "He knows I'll do anything to help our army if the war turns against them. Maybe he wants to neutralize me."

"Wouldn't you, if you were in his position?" Colonel Oliver asked.

"Unless he has something else up his sleeve."

Darien gratefully dismissed the Rat and called in his officers. While he waited for them, he asked Kyle and Anna what they thought.

"I get confused by all the double-dealing," Kyle complained. "It's like you can't trust anybody around here."

"You can't," Darien confirmed. "Marus is surrounded by countries that want our land. Allegiances change almost as quickly as the weather."

"Then what are you going to do?" Anna asked.

"Perhaps we can play both sides for a while," Darien said.

"How?"

A thin smile crept across Darien's face. "We'll give safe delivery of the cannon parts to Monrovia so the baron will get his money. That's what he'll be paying us to do."

Kyle didn't understand. "What good is that?" he asked. "Then the Monrovians will build the cannons and send them to the Palatians."

"How do you suppose they'll get the cannons to the Palatians?" Darien said, pointing to a map hanging on the side of the tent. "They either have to take them south through Gotthard—which Prince Edwin will never allow since he is *our* ally. Or, more likely, they'll transport them by train to the west of Gotthard. That's wide-open wilderness. Anything can happen to those poor trains on the way."

"You'll sabotage the train tracks?" Anna asked.

Darien nodded.

"They'll figure it out eventually," Kyle observed.

"Maybe they will," Darien agreed. "But in the meantime, we'll find the plans to that cannon and get them to our own experts. That'll even things out a little."

The officers entered Darien's tent and wondered why Darien, Anna, and Kyle were smiling.

For nearly three months, the plan worked just as Darien had hoped. While he and his army gave safe conduct to the baron's supplies from Adria to Monrovia, a team of his guerrilla fighters blasted the railway lines west of Gotthard. The Monrovians switched their transportation from trains to trucks and horse-drawn wagons, but the result was the same. No matter how they tried to smuggle the cannons through, Darien's fighters thwarted them. In that time, only six cannons got through to the Palatian front lines, not enough to make a big difference in the war.

One night, in a daring raid, Darien broke into the plant where the Monrovians built the cannons. The blueprints for the cannon were kept in a safe in the president's office. The Rat, who was also skilled as a safecracker, got the safe open. Darien used a new contraption called a *photographic camera* to take pictures of the plans. Then Darien and the Rat crept away, and no one knew they had been there.

Darien had the blueprints delivered anonymously to General Liddell's weaponry office. Darien was quite proud of himself.

In those three months, Kyle and Anna lived with Darien's army in the town of Lizah. It was a mining town settled in an area of Adria where the lush green beauty of the Marus terrain and the Territory of Peace gave way to brown sand, cacti, and dry air. The Marutians found it barren and boring. Darien insisted that Kyle and Anna receive lessons from a tutor; he saw no reason for them to stop learning just because they weren't in their own world. It annoyed Kyle more than Anna, since he disliked doing homework more than she did.

"If I have to go to school and do homework, I may as well be back home!" Kyle pouted. He often felt as though he'd lost his sense of purpose. He didn't get that sick feeling in his stomach anymore, so he had become just another kid in the camp. He didn't like it, and he began to question whether there had ever been an Unseen One to give him the power in the first place.

Anna, on the other hand, studied hard. It wasn't unusual for Kyle to find her reading the Sacred Scroll that Darien had given her or walking and thinking in the wildern ess alone.

"Don't you get bored silly?" he once asked her.

She looked at him with the same indulgent expression their mother often gave him when he'd asked a ridiculous question. "No, I think it's nice out here," she said.

"Okay, so it's nice. But when are we going home?" he asked.

Anna shrugged. She had no idea.

"Don't you care? Aren't you worried about Mom and Dad, Grandma and Grandpa?"

Anna had to think about it before she could answer. "I'm not worried," she replied after a moment. "Somehow the Unseen One will work it all out when we go back."

"*If* we go back," Kyle said. "I don't think the Unseen One is interested—*if* He's even out there."

Anna gazed at her brother for a moment. "You're upset because you don't feel special anymore," she observed.

"What are you talking about?"

"You know what I mean," Anna replied. "Being chosen doesn't mean excitement day in and day out. It doesn't mean we're always being used in obvious ways by the Unseen One. Sometimes it means waiting and being patient and staying faithful."

Kyle folded his arms. "Don't preach at me," he said grumpily.

"You're not sure you believe anymore."

"Leave me alone."

"Can't you believe without that feeling?"

"Oh, that's easy for you to say!" he snapped. "You get those dreams and visions all the time. If the Unseen One gave *me* dreams and visions, I'd believe, too."

Anna shook her head. "I haven't had those dreams in a long time," she said. "But I don't need to have them to believe."

"Well, maybe I do."

"Then you're believing in the wrong thing," she snapped.

"I don't want to talk about it anymore." He turned and walked away from her. She was right in what she said, he knew. The truth was, he felt deserted and rejected by the Unseen One. It was time to take matters into his own hands.

That night, Kyle ventured out from Lizah to see if it would help him think the way Anna thought. The desert evening was cool, so he started a small campfire. He brooded next to it, bugged that he still didn't know what to do to get home. He heard a rustling behind him. Before he could see who it was, the Rat was standing next to him, warming his hands over the fire as if he'd been there all along.

"You scared me," Kyle said in an accusing tone.

"My apologies," the Rat said. "What ails you?"

"Nothing."

"I see you sitting here alone, and I think to myself that you are not happy. Then I think that I am the Rat and able to find things that might make you happy."

"You can't find anything that will make me happy," Kyle said testily.

"Don't be so certain, young protector."

Kyle looked up at him. His eyes looked like embers in the firelight. "I don't have any money. Well, none that you can use."

"On the contrary. You have money from your world."

Kyle frowned. "What do you know about my world?"

"I'm the Rat. I'm supposed to know everything I can. You want to go back to your world. That much I know."

"Yeah, but the Old Judge is dead, and there's nobody else who can help us," Kyle said. He jabbed at the fire with a stick. It spat back at him.

"The Old Judge was not the last of his kind."

"Anna doesn't know how either."

"Anna is not the last of that kind," the Rat said. "There is another. A woman. She can help you."

Kyle brightened up. "Really?"

"I would not say so unless I was sure." The Rat rubbed his hands together and waited.

"Where is she?" Kyle asked. "How can I talk to her?"

The Rat spread his arms. "She's a long way from here. Back in Marus. You'll have to journey a day and a half to get to her."

"I don't care. I'm ready to go."

"Then give me some of your otherworldly money and the Rat will take care of everything."

Kyle dug around in his pocket. He found a couple of dollar bills and 63 cents in change, and he thought he'd better hang on to a dollar.

The Rat smiled as Kyle placed the rest of the money in his palm. "You're too generous," the Rat said. "Meet me here in an hour."

Kyle was beside himself with joy and ran to tell Anna the news.

Anna wasn't in her room. Darien had asked her—and Kyle—to come to the briefing room in his headquarters at what was once a schoolhouse. When no one could find Kyle, Anna went alone. The briefing room (actually, one of the old classrooms) was crowded with officers and the elected leaders of the community. To the left of the podium, Baron Orkzy sat, regal and erect. He could have been the principal for this school. Darien called everyone to silence.

"I have important news. The war with the Palatians is deadlocked," Darien announced. "The Palatians are fed up."

"They're ready to surrender then?" someone asked with a chuckle.

Darien didn't smile. "No. They're ready to conquer. The baron and I met this evening. He tells me the Palatians are calling in all debts from the nations who're friendly to them. As of midnight tonight, the Monrovians are going to join the war on the side of Palatia."

The room erupted in shouts and protests.

Darien waved his arms to get them quiet again. "It's worse than that," he continued. "Many of the leaders of the Adrian tribes are ready to side with Monrovia and Palatia as well."

"Even the baron?" another voice called out.

Darien gestured to the baron. "Please tell them what you told me."

The baron stood up, a giant in the room. "I despise this sort of thing, I have to confess," he began. "I prefer neutrality. It makes for better business. But the Adrian leaders are putting a lot of pressure on me to swear allegiance to Palatia."

"And what about us?" a woman shouted.

"To put it bluntly, they don't trust you," the baron said. "They seem to suspect that you've had something to do with all those nasty explosions on the Monrovian railway lines. Imagine that. They believe that you actively thwarted the delivery of the cannons to the Palatians."

The room was silent. A few knowing smiles were exchanged.

The baron pulled a handkerchief from his sleeve and dabbed the side of his nose. "Naturally, it's none of *my* business since the parts I'd promised to them were delivered. I'd rather *not* know whether you were involved as saboteurs. Now, however, they're forcing me to be involved. They want me to make a decision. And by forcing *me* to make a decision, they're forcing *you* to make a decision."

"What kind of decision?"

"Whether you're going to stay here and behave yourselves, or whether you're going to side with your countrymen." The baron leaned against the podium dramatically. "One will ensure that you live in peace, the other will put you at risk as enemies of our allies."

A wave of murmuring rolled through the gathering.

"I've been told to offer you a deal, though," said the baron.

"What kind of deal?" Colonel Oliver asked from the side of the room.

"Everyone knows of the conflict between King Lawrence

and General Darien. It is also well known that General Darien will likely win out as your next ruler."

Colonel Henri stood up. "What's your point, Baron?" he asked.

The baron looked at the colonel with disdain. "Side with the Palatians and you will be given a significantly large portion of Marus's northern counties. General Darien will be installed as your king. This the Palatians promise to you if they are victorious."

The room erupted again in a commotion of catcalls and dissension.

"You have until tomorrow to decide," the baron said over the noise, and with a grand flourish, he left the room.

Darien returned to the podium and tried to get control of the crowd. Then the arguments among them began. Anna didn't stay. She felt an odd but strong desire to take a walk.

The dream took her by surprise. She hadn't had one in such a long time and had resigned herself to the idea that she might never have one again. But there it was, more vivid and real than any she'd ever had before.

She saw King Lawrence. He was thin and wild-eyed, pacing with his hands clasped behind his back in what looked like a tent. General Liddell stood nearby, a dark and sour expression on his face.

"Well, sire?" Liddell asked.

"I don't know! I don't know! How can I know?" the king cried out.

"A decision—orders to attack—*anything* will be helpful at this time." The anger in General Liddell's voice was unmistakable. "In just a few hours, we'll have not one but *three* enemies to contend with. What do you want us to do?"

The king paced more quickly. "If the Old Judge were here, he'd know. He would tell me what to do. Why did he desert me?"

"Because he's *dead*, sire. That's what happens to people. They die. *We'll* die if you don't make a decision soon."

"That's where you're wrong, General. He's not dead. He's around here somewhere. We just have to pick up the phone and give him a call." The king put his thumb and pinkie against his face as if he were talking into a phone.

General Liddell worked his jaw, clenching and unclenching his teeth. "Of course," he said with open sarcasm. "Why didn't I think of it before?"

"I want our armies to stay right where they are for the time being," the king suddenly commanded. "Don't move. Not an inch, not a muscle. I have to find someone to consult with."

"Like who?" General Liddell looked as if he might slap the king if he mentioned the Old Judge again.

"There's a woman. I don't remember her name. She has the power. We'll visit her, and she'll tell us what to do."

"A woman?"

"Yes, yes. Don't be so thick. She lives near . . . Dorr. That's it. I can find her if we go there." The king stopped pacing and leaned over a table with a map on it. He pointed. "That little town right there."

General Liddell didn't bother to look. "You're going to leave your troops *now*? Sire, with all due respect, if they see you leave, they'll panic."

"They won't see me leave. We'll disguise ourselves. That's what we'll do. We'll disguise ourselves, go to the woman, then come back. Just tell the men that we're in conference and can't be disturbed."

"Sire, please—"

"No! Stop arguing with me!" the king screamed. "We have to go! We have no hope of winning if we don't go!"

Anna woke up, alone in the desert. Something made a chirping noise nearby. An owl hooted.

Was this a dream to report to Darien? She wondered. Nothing in it would help them with their decision to stay in Adria or join the king's troops. Then again, maybe she simply couldn't see it. She made her way back to Darien's headquarters. It was deserted except for Colonel Oliver, who was locking the door. He informed her that General Darien had gone off somewhere to think and pray. Whatever she had to tell him would have to wait until morning.

She thanked him and walked to the room she shared with Kyle at the Lizah Hotel. It was dark.

"Kyle?" she called out as she lit a lamp. "Are you here?"

She looked around, her hand brushing against a piece of paper on the table in front of her. It was a note from Kyle.

"I've gone to see someone who will help us get home," the note said in his distinctive cursive. "I'll be back in a couple of days. Then we'll go home!" He had underlined *go home* in heavy strokes.

Anna sat down in a chair and buried her face in her hands.

CHAPTER

17

The sun hadn't fully risen yet when someone knocked on the door. Anna, who hadn't slept all night and was still fully dressed, padded across the room.

"Who is it?" she asked.

"Darien," the familiar voice said.

She opened the door, and before he could say anything she thrust Kyle's note into his hands. He read it, then frowned. "He needs a good kick in his backside," he growled. "It's the wrong day to do something like this."

"You made a decision?"

"I think so," Darien replied. "Unless you have a message for me. Have you had any dreams lately?"

Anna told him about the dream of King Lawrence.

"What am I supposed to make of that?" he asked.

"I don't know," Anna said, distressed.

Darien went to the window and looked out on the street. Colonel Oliver was beginning to assemble the officers and community leaders below. "Your dream may be the confirmation of my decision. The king is obviously losing his grip. He's not capable of fighting the combined allied armies. He needs our help."

"No," Anna said. "That may not be the message at all.

Maybe it means to stay away. Maybe you should wait until—"

"Until what, Anna?" he shouted at her. "Until the Palatians have conquered our country?"

She winced as if he'd struck her in the face, her eyes tearing up.

He checked himself and continued more quietly. "What you mean is that you want me to wait until Kyle comes back. I can't do that. Whatever we do, we have to do quickly. Right now."

"I understand," Anna whispered.

"I've decided that we won't stay here. All the civilians will go back to where we camped in the Territory of Peace. You'll be as safe there as anywhere."

"What about your army?"

"We're going south to join the royal army," Darien said. "We have to help them fight against the Palatians. It'll be a massacre otherwise."

"What if King Lawrence has you arrested—or you're killed?" Anna asked.

"Then we've all been terribly misled and the Unseen One didn't really choose me to be king."

—⚙—

The Rat and Kyle took a night train from Lizah to Krawley. From there they caught a train that took them south to Sarum. They arrived the next morning, just in time for a connecting train to Dorr. Kyle slept most of the way, though he awoke with a sick feeling in the pit of his stomach.

"I hope I didn't make a big mistake," he said.

"Do you think it would be a mistake to find your way home?" the Rat asked.

Kyle didn't answer.

The Rat glanced at a map on the wall of the Dorr station. "Only a few miles' walk," he said, "then you'll have your answer."

An hour later, they passed the post office for Wollet-in-Stone. "I know this place," Kyle said. "This is where we picked up Anna after she escaped from the convent!"

Five minutes later, they were standing outside a wooden shack with a tin roof. A red palm was painted on the doorway. "That's the sign of a seer," the Rat said. He knocked on the frame since the door was hanging wide open. "Hello?" he called.

Someone shuffled and banged inside, as if the person had been startled and tipped something over. An old woman, older than any Kyle had ever seen, appeared in the doorway, wiping her hands on the skirt of her peasant dress. A tattered shawl hung like cobwebs from her shoulders. "Yes? Anastasia, I am," she said. "What can I do's for ye?"

"The boy needs to talk to you," the Rat explained. "About matters of another world."

"Come in and sit ye down! Sit ye down!" she said, clearly delighted.

Kyle followed her in and immediately regretted it. The place was a dump. The woman scooted a skeletal cat from one of the chairs and positioned it next to the table in the center of the shack. Kyle reluctantly sat down, then noticed that the Rat hadn't joined them. He stood in the doorway.

"Come in," Kyle said.

"This is your affair, not mine," the Rat said. "I'll meet you at the station when you're done."

Before Kyle could say anything, the Rat was gone.

"Matters of another world?" Anastasia asked.

Kyle surveyed the room. Besides the obvious dirt and trash, he noticed an old, faded carnival poster hanging on the wall. "Anastasia the Mysterious" the headline read in large, curly letters. The woman in the painting bore little resemblance to the old, shriveled person in front of him, however. That woman was dark and beautiful, with wild hair and eyes that probably caught the hearts of many men.

Anastasia cleared her throat. Her hand was held out for payment.

"Oh, sorry," Kyle said. He dug into his pocket, found his last dollar, and gave it to her. "I hope that's enough."

She held up the greenback and giggled. "Money from the other world. Oh yes. I'll add it to my collection, I will." She opened a small tin confectioner's box. Kyle thought he caught sight of an American nickel before she shoved the dollar in and closed the box up tight.

"I want to go home," Kyle said when Anastasia turned her attention to him once more.

"Home! Yes, yes. We all want to go home. Give me yer hand."

He held out his hand to her. She took it quickly, then just as quickly let it go. Her face looked as if she'd been jolted with electricity. "No. Ye are tricking me, ye are."

Kyle was confused. "What do you mean?" he asked.

The old woman had the tin box open again and was fumbling around for the dollar. "Ye are not true. Ye should not be here, no." She threw the dollar back at him. "Go! Hurry!"

"What's wrong?" Kyle asked as Anastasia came around the table and nearly pulled him from the chair. "You're supposed to help me."

"I cannot help ye. No. Why didn't ye tell me ye were a chosen protector? Are ye trying to kill me?" She pushed him to the door, stopping only when the sound of approaching horses could be heard above her gravelly commotion.

"Tell you—" Kyle was bewildered.

"It's too late!" the woman cried. "It's too late!"

The horses were reined to a stop next to the shack. Two men dressed in what looked like monks' hoods climbed off and strode toward the door. The woman stumbled backward and slumped into her chair. Kyle looked at Anastasia, then back at the two men. They yanked their hoods off. King Lawrence and General Liddell walked in.

"Oh no . . ." Kyle said.

"Oh yes," General Liddell replied, then backhanded him. Kyle was halfway to the ground when Liddell grabbed him and yanked him back to his feet. Dazed, Kyle tried to speak, but he couldn't. He felt a sliver of warm blood trickle from his mouth.

"Do you know this boy?" King Lawrence asked.

"Don't you remember him?" Liddell replied. "He was with Darien."

The king's eyes came alive. "Is he the boy they keep talking about? The one who keeps saving Darien's life?"

"Saved him from my marksman in the Territory of Peace," General Liddell growled.

"I remember now. We met at the palace. Or at the Old Judge's cottage. Or somewhere. How nice to meet you again," King Lawrence said with a smile. "Your timing couldn't be better."

"He'll make a wonderful hostage," Liddell said.

The king glared at his general. "Hostage! You're mistaken, my friend. He will be my aid and my assistant!"

"Sire—"

The king continued, "He'll be *my* protector. My own lucky

charm! If he saved Darien, he can save me! This is wonderful!" The king's face was aglow, like a child who's just found
all the answers to an important test ahead of time. Then he
suddenly looked confused. "But what's he doing here?"

"Nothing, my lord," Anastasia said. "We were just chatting, that's all. Talking, we were. Passing time away, la-di-da."

The king pushed Kyle toward a chair. "Sit down, my
protector," he ordered. "Your visit here may be—*must be*—
providential. You may give this old charlatan a little help. A
boost for her failing powers!" He laughed, pulled up another
chair, and sat down.

He's insane, Kyle thought. *The king has gone completely
over the edge.*

Anastasia said fearfully, "Powers, my lord? I'm just an old
woman trying to make her way through life. What powers?"

"Oh, be quiet," General Liddell said. "We know what
you are, though I don't believe in it myself. The king wants
your advice."

The king cocked an eye at her. "You don't think I know
what the red palm means? You think I don't know about you?
I'm the king of this country, and I *know*." He brought his fist
down against the rickety old table. It nearly collapsed. "Now
tell me what I must do! Tell me and *be right,* blast you!"

Anastasia fumbled around for a moment, picking up
a deck of cards, then putting them down again. She then
reached for a small gold pendant, thought better of it, and
put it back. "I'll need a moment, I will."

"*Now,* hag," General Liddell said from his place by the door.

Anastasia had a new idea. "Dark," she said. "It must be
dark. Close the door, you must. Pull the drapes."

"You pull the drapes," Liddell said as he closed the door.
"I wouldn't touch them with a 10-foot barge pole."

"Pull the drapes, General!" the king shouted.

Liddell obeyed grudgingly. The shack was now in a hazy darkness. Light still peeked through the spaces and holes in the wall's wooden planks.

"What now?" the king asked.

"Close your eyes," she said nervously.

She's stalling, Kyle thought. He wiped the side of his mouth, which now felt numb. The bleeding had stopped. Through his half-closed eyes, he looked around to see if there was any way to escape. Liddell was still standing next to the door. The only door. There was no other way out.

"What do ye want to know?" Anastasia asked.

"Will I be victorious against the Palatians?" King Lawrence asked.

The old woman stammered, "The Palatians. Oh, yes. Them. Victorious. Well . . . I think . . ."

"I don't care what you think!" the king growled. "I want you to ask *him.*"

"Who?"

"The Old Judge!"

"No . . . please. I can't call the Old Judge. Calling him would be like . . . like . . ."

"Asking for the Unseen One?" the king said. "Yes, I know. Now call him! He'll tell me what I need to know. Say his name."

"No!" Anastasia cried.

King Lawrence reached across the table and grabbed her by the throat. "Say his name!"

"No one has said his name in years!" she shrieked.

"Say it!" he screamed at her. "Say it! Say the name!"

Anastasia gasped as the king tightened his grip around her throat. She had to say the name or die, that much was certain. So she said it in a hoarse whisper. "Samuel."

"Louder!"

"Samuel!" she screeched.

The king let her go and looked around. "Now what?"

She whimpered and fell from the chair to her knees. "No!"

"What do you see?"

"It's rising from the earth," she said. "An old man in a cloak."

The king spun around. "Where? I don't see it."

Kyle had no idea if what he saw next was something that appeared to his eyes or to some other senses, but it was definitely the Old Judge. But he didn't appear like a ghost or a spirit, nor did he appear as a living person. He was a presence that seemed to fill the room, standing at all points simultaneously, no matter which way one turned.

"Why are you troubling me?" the Old Judge asked, annoyed.

The king's voice trembled, not from fear but from relief. "Ah!" he said. "The Palatians are going to attack, and I don't know what to do. You were my last friend—my only friend—and I need your help. Tell me what the Unseen One wants me to do."

"Why do you ask me now?" the Old Judge asked. "I have told you all there is to know. You have turned your back on the Unseen One, and so He has taken the kingdom from your hands and given it to another. You have not obeyed. You have not believed. You did not remain faithful. Now it is too late. You have led the people of Marus to disaster. Death waits for you!"

The king threw himself to the ground. "No, Samuel! No! Save me! You must save me! Samuel!"

The Old Judge held up his hand. "Speak my name no

more," he commanded. Then it was as if he turned to Kyle, though he didn't actually move, and he said, "You are in bad company, boy. You should have had faith. You should have been patient."

"I know, but—"

The door suddenly blew open, the curtains were ripped from their flimsy rods, and light poured in. They all covered their eyes and, when they could see again, the shack was as it had been when they arrived. The Old Judge was gone, leaving only a trace in the memory that he had ever been there at all.

General Liddell was obviously shaken. He helped King Lawrence to his feet. "Sire, we must go," he said.

"Yes, we must," the king agreed.

Kyle considered making a dash for the door, but the two men blocked the way. General Liddell guided the king out, and Kyle hoped they had forgotten him. Suddenly the king reached back, catching Kyle by the shoulder. "You're coming with us," King Lawrence snarled. "Your power as protector might be greater than his power as a prophet."

"No!" Kyle cried, struggling against him.

The king leered at him, madness gathering like foam at the corners of his mouth. "You'll be my lucky charm!" he shouted.

General Darien and his soldiers had left to fight the Palatians. Anna, along with the rest of the civilians, packed a few provisions for the journey back to the Territory of Peace. She had just put her hands on a few of Kyle's belongings when the vision came. It hit her like a lightning bolt, and she fell to the floor. She saw Anastasia's shack, and in it were Anastasia, King Lawrence, General Liddell, Kyle, and the Old Judge. She heard every word of condemnation the Old Judge passed on to the king. She felt the burning fury of the Old Judge's anger. Yet behind it, she also felt sadness and disappointment.

Then it was gone.

Her mind raced to interpret what she'd seen. Surely it wasn't real. How could the Old Judge, who was dead, be in the shack with the king and General Liddell? And what was Kyle doing there? The dream was all mixed up, as if someone had thrown images together in the wrong place. *It wasn't a dream,* she decided. *I'm just worried about Kyle.*

From outside, she heard a shot and a scream. Then the sound of horses' hooves came in like thunder. *Another dream?* she wondered as she looked out the window.

It wasn't a dream. The Adrians were attacking.

CHAPTER

18

Gathered together in the Lizah Hotel, Anna and the rest of the civilians—some 200 people in all—found themselves guarded by Adrian soldiers. Apart from being pushed and shoved, no one was hurt. One of the community leaders, an old man named Morlock, demanded to know why they were being held. The guards refused to answer; instead they gestured with their guns.

Early afternoon, a commotion arose by the hotel front door. A moment later, Baron Orkzy walked in. His normal composure was replaced by breathless worry. His hair was tousled, his clothes askew. He'd obviously been manhandled, though Anna couldn't imagine anyone being large enough to do such a job.

The baron asked everyone to gather around. Then he addressed them, punctuating his comments with flutters of his handkerchief. "Ladies and gentlemen, I've been asked to explain your situation," he said. "As it stands now, you're being held hostage."

"Tell us something we don't know," Morlock snapped.

"Please don't interrupt," the baron replied wearily. "You're being held hostage as a bargaining tool. General Darien will be intercepted and given a message from my Adrian rulers. Essentially, the message will inform him that if he does not return to Lizah immediately, you will all be killed."

Several women cried out. Someone began to sob.

"Now, now, none of that," the baron said. "My Adrian leaders aren't really interested in hurting you."

"What *are* they interested in?" Morlock asked.

"They're interested in keeping General Darien and his soldiers from helping King Lawrence. By using you as collateral, they have a good chance of succeeding."

Morlock refused to yield. "What makes you so sure General Darien will come back? He may choose his duty to the king over our lives."

The baron sniffed. "That would be most regrettable since, if he doesn't return, you *will* die."

Morlock quickly stepped forward, a knife in his hand. "What will stop us from taking *you* hostage?"

The baron looked at Morlock's face, down at the knife, then back at his face. "You old fool," he said angrily, "I'm already a hostage! Don't you understand? This whole business wasn't *my* idea. I'm only the messenger. Now I have to wait here with you for Darien's return. So put that little blade away like a nice little man, and stop being so overdramatic."

Morlock's face turned red against his white beard, but he put the knife away. "What do we do now?" he asked glumly.

"Wait for Darien's answer," the baron said. "And hope that this hotel has decent coffee."

A couple of hours passed. Anna sat alone in a red velvet chair to the side of the hotel lobby. She read portions of the Sacred Scroll, prayed, then read some more. She dreamed without sleeping, a variety of images clearly presented and understood.

A blast of cologne suddenly filled her nostrils, and she looked up. The baron stood over her.

"May I sit with you for a moment?" he asked.

"Yes, sir," she said.

He sat down next to her. Even then he was as tall as she. "You're one of those . . . oh, what do they call them? A *voice*. For the Unseen One. Do you know what Darien will do?"

Anna did. She had already seen the Adrian messenger stop Darien and the troops. She decided not to say so, though. "General Darien is torn between his duty to the king and his love for the people here," she offered.

"I know that," the baron said. "But will he come?"

"I cannot answer that," Anna replied.

"Because you don't know or because you won't say?"

Anna gazed at him without answering.

The baron examined his fingernails for a moment. Then he asked, "What will become of the king?"

Anna's heart ached, as if somehow she shared in the pain and disappointment the Unseen One felt at that moment, like a father who had to punish a rebellious child. "The king will suffer the full consequences of his faithlessness."

The baron let the subject drop. Then, as if he'd just remembered something else, he said, "You have a brother. Where is he? Did he go with Darien?"

"No," Anna said, her eyes starting to burn. "He is with the king."

The baron lifted his eyebrows. "Oh, dear. What will happen to him?"

"He will go home."

The battle against the Palatians was a catastrophe from the start. King Lawrence ignored his generals' advice to spread his battalions out over strategic areas to the south, west, and north of Kellen. He thought they would be more effective as one solid army, concentrating on the Palatian troops to the west. This allowed the Palatians to circle from the south and southwest, while the Monrovians and Adrians circled in from the north and northwest. Prince Edwin of Gotthard hastily assembled his army and cut off part of the Monrovian and Adrian forces, but it wasn't enough.

King Lawrence found himself outflanked and outmaneuvered in the Valley of the Rocks. Where he had once trapped General Darien, he was now himself trapped. The Palatians bombarded the king and his soldiers with cannon fire, then moved in for hand-to-hand combat.

Kyle witnessed it all firsthand. The king would not let Kyle out of his sight after they left Anastasia's shack. "You're my lucky charm," he said over and over.

Kyle explained in despair that he wasn't anyone's lucky charm. "I'm just a kid," he insisted.

"You protected General Darien," the king said. "You'll protect me."

"I can't," Kyle pleaded. But his words had no effect. The king dressed Kyle as one of his attendants and insisted that the boy stay nearby wherever he went. That included the battle against the Palatians.

The Palatians broke through the front lines of the Marutian army and aggressively made their way along the edges of the Valley of the Rocks toward the Royal Guards—those who were committed to protecting the king. The Royal Guards fell quickly at the hands of the Palatians. The king's sons, including Prince George, rushed to counterattack. Kyle saw the Palatians strike them down.

King Lawrence watched from his hiding place, his sword drawn. "Tell me what to do!" he commanded Kyle.

"I don't know!" Kyle cried.

The king grabbed him. "Then we'll run."

Blindly, they stumbled through the passages and crevices of the rocks, the roar of cannons and gunfire in their ears. No matter how far they went, however, the Palatians' shouts seemed close behind. Somehow they wound up at the very cave that Darien had found months before. It seemed like such a long time ago, Kyle thought.

"Maybe they won't find us here," the king said breathlessly, panic in his eyes.

Kyle fell to the floor of the cave. It was muddy and cold. "Help me!" he prayed to the Unseen One. "I don't deserve it, but please help me."

The Palatians were coming. Kyle could hear their voices echoing in the rocks around the cave.

"Tell me," the king said to Kyle, "are we safe here?"

Kyle shook his head and began to cry. "I don't know!" he said.

The king slapped him. "Prophesy for me! You're supposed to be my protector! Tell me your dreams!"

Kyle put his face in his hands.

The Palatians weren't far from the mouth of the cave now. Kyle felt sick to his stomach, but it wasn't a warning. He knew they were doomed.

The king looked around, wild-eyed. "They can't capture me!" he shouted. "They'll humiliate me—torture me. I can't be captured!" He thrust his sword handle at Kyle. "As soon as they arrive, you have to kill me."

"No!" Kyle said, pushing the handle away. "I won't."

"You have to!" King Lawrence demanded.

Kyle refused.

Just then, a Palatian soldier appeared at the mouth of the cave. King Lawrence drew his pistol and shot him. Kyle scrambled behind a nearby rock for cover.

"You won't have me!" the king shouted to the Palatians.

He followed Kyle and begged, "Please, take my life! Don't let me die in dishonor!"

Kyle looked helplessly at the king. "No. I can't!"

The king leaned against the cave wall, looking like a puppet that someone had casually thrown there. "This is the end," he said mournfully. "Oh, that it should come to this!" A tear slid down his face. "This is what it's like to die as a coward, without faith. May the Unseen One forgive me." He lifted the pistol and put it to the side of his head.

Kyle realized too late what was about to happen. He turned away as the king pulled the trigger. The sound of the blast exploded through the cave.

Kyle didn't remember much after that. He crawled away from the king on his hands and knees, the mud on the cave floor sticking to him like tar. His body convulsed from his sobs. With little strength left, he got to his feet. The Palatians were in the cave now. One raised the butt of his rifle and brought it crashing down on Kyle's back. The pain shot through his body and he thought, *This is what it's like to die as a coward. Without faith.* His mind was filled with images of pirates and adventure, of abandoned houses and a room with whispering voices, of guardian angels and being chosen by the Unseen One. *I was going to be a hero*, he thought. *But I didn't have patience. I didn't have faith.*

He closed his eyes as stars spun in his head. For a moment he thought he saw Anna peering at him through a hole in a ceiling.

Anna didn't tell Baron Orkzy what Darien had decided because she didn't want to spoil the element of surprise. She feared that the baron might blab to the Adrians that Darien was coming back to rescue them. As it turned out, the baron had bribed one of the guards and departed long before Darien's return.

Darien and his army didn't approach Lizah by the normal route. They circled around the south of the town, to the west, and caught the Adrian soldiers completely unawares. Darien's attack was swift and merciless. The Adrians who managed to escape told of the "mad Marutian general" for years to come. Others called it "Darien's Fury."

Darien never forgave the Adrians for the deception that took him away from the king in his hour of need.

Anna was still sitting in the red, velvet chair in the lobby of the Lizah Hotel when Darien and a handful of men burst in. The hostages cheered him. He ignored them and went straight to Anna. He knelt in front of her, his face dripping with sweat, his eyes a picture of worry.

"Well?" he asked.

"The king is dead," she said in a voice that seemed far, far away.

Darien lowered his head. When he looked up again, the sweat had been replaced with tears. They traced lines through the dust on his cheeks.

Colonel Oliver suddenly joined them. "General, we just heard on the shortwave," he said. "Our armies were defeated. Prince George was fatally wounded . . . and the king has been killed."

Somewhere in the room, a shout of joy went up.

Darien leaped to his feet and furiously cried out, "No! Be quiet, all of you! There'll be no joy. We'll have no celebration. The king—God's chosen—is dead. Let there be mourning and lamentation. Our king is dead."

The crowd was silenced, and the people slowly made their way out of the hotel.

"We must go to Sarum," Colonel Oliver said softly to Darien. "The nation needs your leadership now."

Darien looked at Anna. "Is it true?" he asked.

Anna nodded. "You are the king now."

"Will we be victorious over the Palatians?"

"You will, but at a great cost."

Darien gazed at her for a moment. "You're not going back to Sarum with me, are you?"

She shook her head slowly. "I'm going to find Kyle."

Darien didn't understand. He couldn't have. But he accepted it anyway. Kneeling again, he kissed her hand. "May the Unseen One allow us to meet again," he said softly.

She smiled at him. She hoped He would.

Darien and Colonel Oliver strode quickly from the hotel. Anna was alone. She felt a heaviness in her heart that seemed to weigh down her feet as well. She stood and walked sluggishly up the stairs to her room. She wasn't sure what she would find there, but she felt compelled to go.

Opening the door to her room, she saw that it was different. "Oh," she said. The furniture and carpets were gone, replaced by broken boards, peeling wallpaper, and dirt. A white light flashed, grew in intensity, and seemed to swallow her up.

CHAPTER

Anna was on her hands and knees in the bedroom at the abandoned house in Odyssey. Somewhere, someone was groaning. She followed the sound to the door. Careful to avoid the section of the floor that had collapsed, she peeked through a large hole to the floor below. Kyle was lying there on his back. He was wearing his normal clothes. He moved his head slightly and groaned some more.

"Kyle!" she called out.

He didn't answer.

Anna navigated the upstairs hallway back to the stairs. She took them two at a time, then raced into the room where Kyle still lay, semiconscious from the fall.

"Don't move," she whispered in his ear. "I'll get help."

The little sister who had seemed to hate adventure and screamed at bugs ran with all her might back through the woods. How she found her way to her grandparents, she didn't know, but she did.

"What in the world . . . ?" her grandmother asked when Anna burst through the back door into the kitchen.

"In the woods—" Anna gasped, her breathlessness getting in the way of her words.

Her grandmother shook her head. "Calm down, child,"

she said. "Take a deep breath while I get you some lemonade."

"But Grandma—"

"I knew going to those woods was a bad idea," Grandma said as she started to pour a glass of lemonade. "I figured you were gone an awful long time. Two hours was long enough, but when it got to be three, well . . ." She *tsked* with her tongue.

"Three hours?" Anna said, shocked. "But we've been gone for months and months!"

"Don't exaggerate," Grandma scolded. "Now, where's your brother?"

"That's what I'm trying to tell you!" Anna cried out. "He's hurt!"

Grandma nearly dropped the pitcher of lemonade. Then, quickly regaining her composure, she shouted for Anna's grandfather to come quickly. Anna told them both about Kyle's fall. Grandma called an ambulance while Anna and Grandpa retraced Anna's steps to the abandoned house.

Kyle was kept in the Odyssey hospital overnight. His back was bruised, and the doctors were worried that he might have fractured a rib in the fall. More than that, though, they wanted to be certain he didn't have a concussion. He seemed delirious when the ambulance brought him in. He kept talking about Darien, King Lawrence, and "a protector."

That evening, Anna sat alone with Kyle in his room. They didn't speak at first but seemed to scrutinize the room as if they'd never seen anything like it before. The silver metal on the bed frame above his head reflected the room in distorted shapes. The sheets on the bed were crisp and clean and smelled of detergent. A radio on the bedside table played a song by Doris Day. This was Odyssey. This was America. It was 1958.

He looked into her eyes. "They aren't different colors anymore," he finally said.

"I know."

"Was it a dream?" he asked.

Anna shrugged. "It seems like it now."

He looked away from her, and Anna thought he might cry. "I failed," he said miserably. "I stopped believing. I should've listened to you and waited."

Anna put her hand on his arm.

"I liked being a big shot," he said. "But I forgot who made me what I was."

A slight smile crossed Anna's face. Her brother seemed bigger, much older somehow.

He faced her again. "Are we still chosen?" he asked. "I mean, does it work that way here?"

Her gaze moved upward to a symbol above the bed—a cross. "Yeah," she said. "The Unseen One is here. We're chosen."

"But . . . for what?"

Anna shrugged. "That's what we're going to have to figure out. We were chosen for one thing in Marus. Maybe we're chosen for something else here."

They sat quietly together and thought about it until the nurse said it was time for lights out.

That night, Anna slept without dreams.

Whit closed the notebook and drummed his fingers on the top for a moment. The fire had nearly gone out. The snow had piled up outside. He had half a mug of tea left that was now cold. With no idea what time it was, he picked up the phone and called Jack. They arranged to meet the next afternoon if the roads were clear enough.

"So what do you think?" Jack asked when they saw each other at Whit's End the next day.

"It's a remarkable story," Whit said.

Jack nodded. "Familiar, too."

"Yes, familiar." Whit watched a snowplow drive down the street in front of his shop. "Do you believe it?"

"You mean, do I think it's true?" Jack asked, then shrugged. "What do *you* think?"

Whit lightly stroked his mustache. "I think I want to find out who wrote it."

"I suppose we could go out to the estate where I got the

trunk. Maybe someone knows something about it."

"It's worth asking," Whit said.

The two men put on their coats and walked out the front door. Whit locked up. *There'll be no business today,* he thought. *The kids will be playing in the snow.*

As they carefully stepped onto the slippery sidewalk, Jack said, "This could turn into a nice little adventure."

"I hope so," Whit said, turning up the collar on his coat. "It's a good day to chase after a mystery."

Jack agreed.

And the two of them left to do just that.

And now, *a preview of the* exciting Passages, Book 2

ARIN'S JUDGMENT

In Arin's Judgment, Mr. Whittaker and his friend Jack Allen find another school notebook telling of an adventurous trip from Odyssey to the land of Marus! This time, the traveler is a boy named Wade Mullens, who finds himself in the hands of a man who wants Wade's help in building a powerful weapon to use against his enemies.

The excitement begins in 1945 at the end of World War II, when a friend lets young Wade in on an amazing secret . . .

"Look what my cousin sent me," Bobby said quietly. He looked around the room and out the window, then double-checked to make sure his sister was gone before spreading some pages out on his desk. On them were rough drawings of what looked like a large bomb.

"What are these?" Wade asked.

"Top secret," Bobby said.

"Top secret?"

Bobby's voice fell to a whisper. "This is from my cousin Lee in *New Mexico.*"

"So?"

"So! New Mexico is where they've been working on the atomic bomb."

Wade looked from Bobby's face to the pages, then back to Bobby's face again. "You mean . . .?"

"My cousin Lee's dad—my Uncle Walter—is a scientist who's been working on the atomic bomb. Lee made these drawings from some papers and photos he'd seen in his dad's briefcase."

Wade's heart lurched. "Are you crazy?" he asked breathlessly. "There are spies out there who'd *kill* to get their hands on stuff like this."

"Yeah, I know," Bobby said. "Why do you think I'm being so careful?"

Wade pointed to the next page. "What's all this stuff?"

"I think it's how they make them. See?"

Wade glanced over the list: "Uranium 235 . . . Uranium 238 . . . plutonium . . . nuclear fission . . . isotopes . . . altimeter . . . air pressure detonator . . . detonating head . . . Urea nitrate . . . lead shield . . ."

"Lee said he scribbled down everything he could," Bobby explained.

Wade's mouth was hanging open now. He read about how the various components interacted to cause an explosion. He also saw a page about the effects of radiation on human subjects after the bombs exploded. Many were burned, and some got sick and died. It also warned of radiation getting into water systems and sources of food. "We shouldn't be seeing this," he said finally.

"I know," Bobby said, smiling. "That's why I showed it to you."

"We have to get rid of it."

"I figured I'd throw it in the furnace as soon as we looked

it over," Bobby agreed. "Uncle Walt would put Lee on restriction for the rest of his life if he knew Lee had mailed this to me."

Suddenly a voice at the door said, "Bobby?" It was his mother. The door handle turned. Acting quickly, Bobby grabbed and folded the sheets of paper and shoved them under Wade's untucked shirt. "What's going on in here?" Bobby's mother asked.

"Nothing," Bobby answered with a voice that said just the opposite.

His mother eyed him suspiciously, then looked at Wade. "Good heavens! What happened to you?" she said. "Is that a black eye?"

Wade stammered incoherently.

"He fell down on the way home from school," Bobby lied.

"Looks more like you were in a fight," his mother said. "I think you should go home right away."

"But—" Bobby started to protest.

"No 'buts' about it." She put a hand on Wade's shoulder and guided him out of the room. "You go home and get that eye looked at," she instructed him.

Bobby's mother stayed with Wade all the way down the stairs to the front door. He tried to think of a way to get the papers back to Bobby, but Bobby's mother was in the way the entire time. She handed him his jacket and books. Bobby shrugged helplessly at Wade as Wade walked through the door and it closed between them.

On the front porch, Wade zipped up his jacket and pressed his books to his chest. He could feel the papers under his shirt. He looked around nervously. What if there were spies watching him? What if the government found out that Lee had sent the drawings to Bobby and secret agents were coming to arrest them even now? Wade swallowed hard and walked quickly down the steps of the front porch and out onto the street. His walk soon became a run as he took off for home.

Every casual glance from people he passed by took on sinister meaning. *They know about the papers,* he kept thinking. A large black sedan drove past, then suddenly pulled up next to him. *It's them! It's the agents!* Wade thought. The door opened, and Wade cried out—then blushed with embarrassment as an elderly woman got out of the car to put a letter in the curbside mailbox.

He ducked down some back alleys and zigzagged through his neighborhood, just to make sure he wasn't being followed. When he finally reached his own home, he burst through the front door and raced up the stairs to his room.

"Wade?" his mother called from the kitchen.

Wade dropped the books on his bed, pulled out the papers, and then shoved them under his mattress. It was the only place he could think to hide them on the spur of the moment.

PASSAGES™

Darien's Rise
An epic audio drama based on the book

Adventures in Odyssey's Passages series is designed to retell Bible stories in a new and creative way.

All of these stories are based on key historical events in the Bible. The names were changed, the details altered, and the setting moved to the exciting land of Marus, but as you listen, you may recognize the basic outlines, key characters, and scriptural lessons from these Bible stories.

Arin's Judgment

One minute, Wade Mullens was in Odyssey attempting to burn his top secret drawings for the atomic bomb. The next he knew, he was staring at a man he didn't know, from a time period centuries before.

Wade says this strange prophet is the final sign—an end-time omen of a culture on the verge of annihilation. But a crazed tyrant sees opportunity in Wade—a boy who will usher in a new age of power, thanks to his bomb-making capabilities.

Can Wade stop the reign of terror that the madman's bomb will surely bring? Or is destruction inevitable?

Adventures in ODYSSEY ®

About the author

Paul McCusker is a writer and director for *Adventures in Odyssey* and the award-wvinning Focus On The Family Radio Theatre. He also has written over 50 novels and dramas. Paul likes peanut-butter-and-banana sandwiches and wears his belt backward.

About the illustrator

Mike Harrigan is the art director for Focus on the Family's *Clubhouse* and *Clubhouse Jr.* magazines for kids. He loves the art of visual storytelling and, when he's given the chance, will doodle on just about anything.